Shandra Higheagle Mystery Series

Double Duplicity

Tarnished Remains

Deadly Aim

Murderous Secrets

Killer Descent

Reservation Revenge

Yuletide Slaying

Yuletide Slaying

A Shandra Higheagle Mystery

Paty Jager

Windtree Press
Hillsboro, OR

This is a work of fiction, Names, characters, places, and incidents either are the product of the author's imagination or are used fictitiously, and any resemblance to actual persons living or dead, business establishments, events, or locales, is entirely coincidental.

YULETIDE SLAYING

Contact Information: info@windtreepress.com

Windtree Press
Hillsboro, Oregon
http://windtreepress.com

Cover Art by Christina Keerins
Photos: Canstock.com

Published in the United States of America

ISBN 9781944973254

Thank You:

Chicago Tribune, TribPub, The Crimescene Yahoo group, and my son-in-law. Without all these resources, I wouldn't have been able to capture the story I envisioned.

Chapter One

Shandra Higheagle stood beside Colleen Greer, her boyfriend's mother, feeling like a proud parent. Sheba, her one hundred and twenty pound mutt, was harnessed to the sleigh filled with presents to be given to the foster children attending the fundraiser parade this evening. The tri-colored Newfoundland/ Border Collie mix dog was lapping up the attention given her by the kids and the adults.

"I'm so happy you agreed to let Sheba pull the sleigh," Mrs. Greer said, waving a hand toward the dog and sled. The street was filling up with parade participants as the organizer lined them up on a side street off the main road through Huckleberry.

"I'm glad you asked. I've never seen Sheba so excited. And she didn't even throw a fit when we put the harness on her." She was proud of her dog. They'd visited retirement homes and hospitals, but this was the first time her furry friend was doing something besides licking hands and being pet.

Colleen glanced around. "I wish Ryan could be here."

The wistfulness in the older woman's voice revealed she held her son in high esteem.

"His job takes him all over the county. I believe he was called to a home invasion this morning." Shandra had listened to his side of the conversation as he'd taken the call. While she understood his job as a detective for the Weippe County Sheriff's Department, she still wished he didn't have to be called out at odd hours and sometimes days at a time. She'd grown accustom to his feet on her coffee table, washing two sets of dishes after a meal, and having someone to snuggle with at night. Since meeting Ryan she'd turned a corner on her solitary life and enjoyed sharing it with him.

"You miss him as much as I do." The sparkle in the older woman's eyes wasn't lost on Shandra. Ryan's mom had been trying to fix them up since the first time they'd met and he'd crossed her off his murder suspect list.

"I do miss him when he's gone. I never know what kind of danger he might be in." She hooked her arm through the other woman's. "How did you manage your worry those years he was in the military and then with the police in Chicago?" She led the woman over to where her daughters, Ryan's two sisters, stood on the sidewalk next to a gingerbread man and a street light festooned with a big red ribbon and large silver star.

"I had to believe in my faith and prayed for him every day." Colleen slipped out of her arm and hugged Bridget, the younger daughter, and Cathleen, who worked at the county dispatch. "I'm so glad you girls and your families could make it."

The grandchildren hugged their grandmother and started tugging on their mothers' coats.

Shandra smiled at the two women whose eyes sparkled with the same speculation as their mother's. "I need to make sure Sheba is ready for the parade." She ducked away before the three women could start grilling her about when she and Ryan were going to get married. No dates had been planned nor an engagement announced. Ryan wouldn't talk about a future until he knew his past wouldn't catch up to him. A past he'd only recently shared with her, and one that kept them both up nights worrying and wondering.

A vintage model car decked out in candy canes pulled into line in front of Sheba. She was to be the tail end of the parade. A man dressed in a Santa suit would walk beside her down the main street of Huckleberry. At the decorated tree in the school yard, they would hand out the gifts to the children. At the playground, various games and fun were keeping the locals and visitors busy until the parade started.

One of Ryan's nephews handed Sheba's leash over to her.

"Thank you. Enjoy the parade," she said, as he trotted off to catch up to his mother, aunt, cousins, and grandmother. She stared at the happy Greer family as they headed down the sidewalk to find a place to watch the parade. All her life she'd wanted a large family and sisters. If she and Ryan married, that wish would be fulfilled. But she didn't need to marry him to have a family. She was now fully involved with her father's family, the Higheagles. She loved her aunt and uncle and all her cousins who lived on the reservation. They had opened their arms and their ways to her, helping her to fully discover herself.

"The parade starts in five minutes!" shouted the man in charge of lining up the entries.

When Colleen first asked Shandra to participate in the parade, she'd balked. Even though she loved Huckleberry and had made it her home, she preferred to live a hermit lifestyle on the mountain. She was happy to spend her days gathering clay, throwing vases that were works of art, and riding her horses. But the parade was for a charity Colleen chaired, and she couldn't turn down Ryan's mom. The charity had picked Huckleberry out of all of Weippe County as the perfect site for the parade. With the ski resort less than ten miles from the town, they'd made sure the event was well publicized at the lodge. Colleen had hopes of getting some of the tourists' money at the winter carnival games.

Shandra spotted the first entries moving down the street. "Where's your Santa?" she asked Sheba, petting her big furry head.

Santa stepped out of a store and hurried over. "I didn't want to stand out in the cold any longer than I had to," the elderly pastor of the nondenominational church in town said.

"I understand." She held the leash out to the man as the vintage car in front of them backfired.

Sheba yelped and took off running down a side street.

"Sheba! Sheba!" Shandra ran after her, but lost sight of the dog as she turned down another street.

She glanced back and caught the backside of Santa walking back to the street.

Yuletide Slaying

What was Colleen going to think when her sleigh full of presents didn't show up at the end of the parade? "I have to find her."

Shandra jogged down the street calling for her dog. "Sheba! Sheba!"

She expected people to step out and wonder who she was calling but from the closed signs in the businesses, it seemed everyone was at the parade. Everyone but her.

"Sheba!" She glanced right and left at each cross street. She didn't see the dog, the red sleigh, or any presents. Where could her furry mutt have disappeared?

She passed the police station and called. "Sheba!"

"Woof! Woof!"

"Sheba, girl, where are you?" she called back and headed down the side street where she'd heard the bark.

Sheba walked out of an alley behind the clinic. She still wore the harness and the sleigh appeared.

Air whooshed out of Shandra's lungs.

A pair of boots connected to legs hung over the edge of the sleigh.

Chapter Two

Shandra grabbed the leash dragging beside her dog and glanced at the body in the sleigh. She didn't know him but that didn't mean anything. Her dealings in Huckleberry only brought a quarter of the population into her world. There was a darker red spot on his red winter coat.

A quick glance up the street revealed the volunteers bustling about getting the carnival games ready at the school grounds. Not a good direction to lead a sleigh holding what appeared to be a dead man. Best to find out if he was still alive. She led Sheba down the street alongside the clinic and up to the emergency door. She pressed the buzzer and waited, scanning the area between the clinic and where she'd found Sheba. Whoever injured this man was out there somewhere. A chill chased up her back.

The doors swished open. Relief washed through her at the sight of Chandler Treat, the emergency nurse. His brother was engaged to one of Shandra's friends.

And he'd tended to her before when someone had tried to run her down in the grocery store parking lot.

"Shandra, good to see you." He glanced at Sheba. "This isn't a vet clinic." He smiled and laughed at his own joke.

"I- She-." Words weren't coming, so she stepped aside and waved to the body in the sleigh.

The nurse's dark face lightened a shade. "Where did you get that?" He stepped by her and grabbed the body's wrist, placing his fingers between the cuff of the winter coat and the thick mitten on the man's hand.

The wide-eyed look and slight shake of Chandler's head told her the man wouldn't see another Christmas.

"Where did you find him?" He keyed in numbers and the emergency doors opened again. "Lead that dog in here so we can get the man out of the sleigh."

"Shouldn't you call the police before you do that?" Even though she didn't want to be connected to another dead body, she knew enough to know that the police needed to see the evidence before the body was moved.

"Good idea." Once they were all inside the clinic, Chandler picked up a phone and dialed.

Shandra wrapped the leash around her hand and then unwound it. Sheba pressed against her, all playfulness gone as her large brown eyes with droopy lids stared at her.

"Yeah, you heard me right. I got a dead body, in a sleigh, in the emergency room." Chandler hung up the phone. "There's days I wonder about the people working on the Huckleberry Police force."

She smiled slightly, remembering her first encounter with Officer Blane. He was a young, first-time officer who had cuffed her and planned on hauling her to the station as the murderer. Ryan's knowledge had kept her out of handcuffs and out of jail.

"Where did you find him?" Chandler asked, walking around the sleigh.

"Sheba found him. A car backfired in the parade line and she took off. I ran down the street calling her name. I lost sight of her. She barked and I followed the sound." She waved a hand. "And found this."

Running feet stopped outside the glass emergency door.

A moan crawled up her throat. Officer Blane.

Chandler hit the button on the inside to open the door and the young man burst into the building. His gaze traveled from her to the body in the sleigh.

"You again!" He started toward her with handcuffs in his hands.

The big ER nurse stepped between her and the officer. "She didn't do it. She brought him here to see if he was still alive."

Blane pulled out his phone. "Chief, we have a body in a sleigh, just like he said." He listened. "Yep." He listened some more. "It's that Higheagle woman and her dog." His head bobbed. "Yes, sir." He closed the conversation and motioned to Shandra to step away from Sheba.

"I need to hold onto my dog." She wrapped her arms around Sheba's neck.

"Let me take a photo, then you can unhitch the dog." Blane pulled out a small camera and took photos from all angles, including Sheba in the photos.

Shandra released the furry neck and stood.

"What the—" Blane stepped toward her with his hand out.

She took a step back.

"Hold still, Shandra." Chandler walked up to her. "Yep, that's blood."

A quick glance at the front of her tan coat showed a red smear.

"That wasn't there when she came in," Chandler quickly stated.

They all dropped their gaze to Sheba.

Shandra lowered to her knees and felt the fur at her dog's neck. One spot was sticky. Fear for Sheba started her heart racing. Had her furry friend tried to defend the man and been hurt in the process? Her fingers moved gently, parting the hair. She found a cut an inch long, oozing blood.

"It's her blood. She's been cut." Shandra ignored the blood on her hands and started to reach for her purse.

"Here." Chandler handed her a gauze.

"Thank you." She pressed the bandage against the wound with one hand and worked the buckles loose on the harness with the other.

Sheba licked her cheek.

"She doesn't appear to be in pain," Chandler said, stepping up and helping remove the harness.

A muffled jazz tune came from her purse. She released the harness and dug for her phone.

Colleen.

She took a deep breath and swiped the screen.

"Hello, Colleen."

"Where are you? And the sleigh with presents? Everyone is headed to the school yard, and I don't have gifts for the children." Her tone was scolding, edged with worry.

"It's a long story. I'm at the emergency clinic."

"Oh my! Are you hurt? Not feeling well?" Colleen's concern for her well-being made her feel warm all over.

"No, I'm not hurt. It's hard to explain. I need to get Sheba to the vet."

"I'll send someone over for the gifts." Colleen shouted, "Conor!"

"No. I mean, I'm not sure the police…" How did she tell the woman her gifts might now be part of a murder investigation.

"Police? What police?"

"Did you say police?" Conor's voice was louder than his mother's.

She heard the phone exchanging hands.

"What is this about the gifts and police?" Ryan's older brother asked.

"I can't really talk about it," she said, watching Blane miming for her to cut the conversation off.

"Where's Ryan?" Conor asked.

"I don't know. I have to go." She hated hanging up on the lawyer, but Blane's face was getting redder by the minute.

"Can I take Sheba to the vet?" she asked the officer in charge.

"No. Not until the chief sends someone to investigate this." Blane sent her a crooked smile. "Don't worry. It won't be your boyfriend. The chief knows you're a suspect."

She glared at the pimply-faced officer. It was getting old having him call her a suspect.

Chandler grabbed her arm. "Come on. Let's take Sheba into an exam room. I'll see if I can do anything for her cut."

Thankful the nurse had a caring personality, she followed him into the closest exam room.

"Can you get her up on the table?" he asked, digging in the drawers along one wall.

She grabbed a chair and placed it beside the bed. "Up," she commanded.

Sheba put her front paws on the chair and used it like a step to jump up onto the bed.

Voices and pounding came from the emergency lobby.

"I'll be right back." Chandler left the room.

Shandra took this time alone to sink onto the chair and wonder at how Sheba had caught a dead man in the sleigh. Did she see the crime? She must have with that cut in her neck. Had the man been stabbed? A mental flash to the dark spot on his coat. Had there been a slit?

The noise out front quieted. Her phone jingled the jazz tune. Colleen.

She heaved a sigh and answered. "I'm sorry. I don't know when—"

"We know what happened. We're outside the emergency room. That scrawny officer won't let us in. I called Ryan."

"You shouldn't have. He can't even work on this case with me involved." Her heart thumped hard against her chest. She wished she and Sheba weren't involved. She was getting tired of being a suspect in a murder investigation.

"Well, he can still get to you and give you support. We'll be at the carnival when they let you go."

"Thank you."

The phone went silent.

Chandler returned. "Chief Marlow is out there now. I think they're calling in the state detectives." He picked up more gauze and walked up to Sheba. "Where was that cut?"

She pointed to the spot on the neck where she'd found the cut.

A tall, wide-bodied man walked into the room. "I see you found another body, Miss Higheagle." Chief Marlow had a deep voice and a get down to business attitude for a chief of a six officer station.

"I didn't find it. Sheba did." She retold her story to the chief.

"Which alley did she come from?" he asked.

"The one behind the clinic." She patted her dog's big foot that hung over the edge of the bed. "I think she either tried to defend the man in the sleigh or startled the person who attacked him. She has a cut on her neck."

The chief leaned in to see the cut Chandler was cleaning.

"It's going to need a couple stitches," the nurse said.

"We'll need photos of that before it's stitched up." Chief Marlowe pointed at the wound. "I'll call Hazel in to take photos. Don't touch it until she's done."

Chandler nodded. "It's not bleeding too much. We can wait."

The chief nodded and left the room.

Shandra's phone played music again.

"You're popular," Chandler said, washing his hands at the small sink.

"I wish I wasn't," she said, noting Ryan was the caller.

Yuletide Slaying

"Hello?" she answered.

"Are you okay?" Were the first words he said.

Tears burned the backs of her eyes.

"Yes. I feel so bad. The presents..." she had let his mother down and in a sense him. They'd discussed whether or not her big goofball of a dog could stay focused long enough to pull the sleigh down the street and to the school yard.

"Forget about the presents. Were you or Sheba hurt?" His caring had caught her heart over a year ago.

"I'm fine. We think whoever killed the man cut Sheba. Chandler is fixing her up as soon as they get photos of the cut." Sticking to the facts helped her keep the tears at bay.

"Was the man stabbed?"

"I don't know. Blane was ready to put cuffs on me, but Chandler stuck up for me." She flashed a smile at Chandler.

He grinned back, his white teeth and white jacket shining like a fluorescent bulb against his coffee colored skin.

"Chief Marlow already called the sheriff and told him to keep me off this case. I'm still working on the burglary, but I'll be at your house tonight. Mom offered to stay with you until I get there."

She heard the worry in his voice, but she had Lil at the ranch. "I won't be alone. Lil will be there until you arrive."

"You know my mom. She won't take no for an answer."

She heard the love and grin in his voice.

"Ok. Maybe, we'll have a party. I'll invite all of your family to my place. None of them have seen it."

He laughed and gathered himself. "You know what that would do to Lil's blood pressure."

She laughed. Ryan always knew how to get her mind off sadness. "I'll call and prepare her."

"Miss Higheagle?"

A state trooper she'd met before, walked into the exam room.

"I have to go. See you tonight." She hung up on Ryan and turned to Detective Stu Whorter. He'd been the detective who'd stepped in when her ex-lover had been found murdered on the ski slope last winter.

"Detective Whorter. I wish I could say it was good to see you." She extended her hand.

"It's cliché but we have to stop meeting like this." He shook her hand.

"I agree." She turned to Sheba. "I'm afraid it's my dog who may be in trouble this time."

"Give me your side of this." He pulled out a notepad and jotted down her repeat of how she came across a body in the sleigh.

"I see. We've gone through the victim's pockets and there wasn't any identification on him. Officer Blane is looking for clues in the alley where you found your dog." He walked up to Sheba with his hand held out.

Her big brown eyes watched him and she sniffed his hand. Her long thick tail thumped on the bed.

"Good girl. I just want to see your wound." He stared at the cut and pulled out his phone. "I'll take some photos for myself." He clicked from different angles and put his phone away.

"You can go as soon as your dog is ready." He walked to the door and stopped. His gaze leveled with hers. "Don't leave the area, we may have more questions."

Her gut squeezed. It was his way of saying she was still a suspect.

Chapter Three

Ryan felt like he'd been gone from Shandra for a week instead of sixteen hours. The home invasion had been burglary. Strange items had been taken. Winter survival equipment, food, and hunting equipment.

Pulling up to Shandra's log home after dark, he smiled. The Christmas lights they'd strung Thanksgiving weekend twinkled a warm welcome. The vehicles parked in front of her house filled him with happiness and dread. He loved his family and had kept his gathering with them limited due to the cloud of his undercover assignment in Chicago. He knew they all meant well, trying to get him and Shandra wed. But they would have to wait and he'd have to dodge all their questions. Poor Shandra, she'd must have been dodging them all evening.

He parked by the barn and smiled at the neatly plowed area. One thing he gave Lil, Shandra's

Yuletide Slaying

employee, credit for was her ability to keep the walking
areas and the road to the house cleared of snow.

Christmas music swallowed him up as he entered
the back door. He shoved out of his boots and coat,
hanging the coat next to Shandra's and placing his
boots next to hers. His heart warmed at the sight of their
things hanging side by side. That's the way he wanted
to keep it for the rest of their lives.

"Uncle Ryan!" shouted Darla, Bridget's middle
child. She ran down the hall and wrapped her arms and
legs around him.

"Hello, squirt." He sniffed. The aroma of lasagna
set his stomach growling.

"You sound like a bear," she said, sliding down his
body and tugging on his hand. "Shandra has a big dog.
Come see."

"I've seen Sheba. I need some food." He slipped
loose of the child's grip and walked into the kitchen.
The sight stirred happiness. Shandra and his mother
were setting food on the kitchen island and chatting.

He walked up behind Shandra and wrapped his
arms around her. They had reserved this type of
affection for only when they were alone, but his mom
had a pretty good idea by now how he felt about the
woman.

Shandra patted his hands. "Glad you could make it
for dinner." Her tone was welcoming, but her body had
stiffened slightly as his arms remained around her
waist.

"He's never been late for dinner a day in his life,"
Mom said, placing a basket of garlic bread on the
island. "I'll go have the kids wash up."

The minute his mom's back was turned, he spun

23

Shandra in his arms and peered into her eyes. "Are you okay?" He knew her well enough to see she wanted him to think so.

"I'm fine." Her arms wrapped around his middle and she hugged him.

She wasn't fine. He could feel it in the small tremors in her body. He hugged her close. "I haven't heard much, but we won't talk about it until later. Enjoy the evening."

"We heard dinner was ready." Conor and his wife, Ryan's ex-girlfriend, Lissa, entered the kitchen.

Shandra spun out of his arms. "Yes. Grab a plate, fill it, and find a seat at the dining room table." She busied herself with pouring drinks.

Ryan didn't like how she was denying her emotions, but now wasn't the time to talk about it. He grabbed a plate, loaded it up, and picked a seat next to his brother at the table.

"You hear anything about what happened?" he asked quietly.

"Not much. Something scared the dog and it took off. Shandra followed, lost her, and when she found the dog, the body was in the sleigh." Conor nudged him. "This is a nice house. But a little far from your work isn't it?"

He frowned at his brother. "What are you getting at?"

"When you two tie the knot, this will be a long commute to work. Any chance she'll move?"

"I'm doing just fine commuting right now and as far as tying the knot. It's on the table, but we're both not ready. Quit pushing." He dug into the food on his plate, only stopping long enough to say hi to his sisters and their husbands. By keeping his head down and eating, he hoped to avoid similar conversations with the rest of his family.

Shandra finally walked out of the kitchen with a plate. His family had left the seat next to him open. She sat down, smiled, and received many compliments on the meal.

"Thank you, but you should thank Lil. She's the one who pulled the lasagna out of the freezer and put it in the oven."

"But this isn't store bought. I saw the dish," Cathleen said, forking a bite into her mouth.

"No. When I'm in between projects, I tend to make things and put them in the freezer. That way I have food that can be placed in the oven and ready without preparation."

"When she's working on a project, she puts in long hours in her studio." Ryan smiled, thinking of the nights he'd go to bed and she'd still be out in the studio working. If he didn't bring her food, she'd go without eating.

"You'll have to show us your studio before we leave," his mom said.

He knew Shandra didn't mind showing her studio to people, but she was in the middle of a project and didn't like to show anyone the progress. Not even him. "It's better to get a tour when it's light out."

Mom frowned at him. "There's lights in the building isn't there?"

"Yes. But it's…"

Shandra put a hand on his arm. "It's okay. I'd love to show your family my studio."

"But the piece you're working on?"

25

"Is covered." She glanced around the table. "And I'm sure your family will respect my privacy and not ask me to remove the cover."

"We'd never dream of not respecting your privacy," Bridget said.

"I don't believe that. Do you?" he asked all the men present.

They all started laughing. Everyone seated at the table knew how insistent and tenacious the Greer women could be when they wanted to know something.

Cathleen crossed her heart with her pointer finger. "We promise we won't pry into your work. Now your love life…" She glanced back and forth between him and Shandra.

Shandra's face reddened and his temper flared.

"When we have something to tell you, we'll do it. For now we're both content with things the way they are." He grasped Shandra's hand and squeezed.

"I'm sorry it bothers you that we aren't jumping into marriage, but we both have our reasons for not making that commitment." She smiled at Ryan. "And I agree that when we do decide, you will be the first to know." She laughed. "Well, I'm guessing my family will be the first to know."

He joined her laughter. His family stared at them as if they were crazy. He understood what she meant, having a cousin with sight and a grandmother who came to her dreams, it was very likely the Higheagles would know before Shandra did.

Changing the subject, even though it meant bringing up Shandra's bad day, he asked, "What happened to the presents for the kids?"

Shandra knew by the way Ryan held her hand, he'd

brought up the day's event to take the marriage questions off of them. Thinking about the man in the sleigh, sent a chill up her spine.

"We salvaged the ones that didn't have…" Colleen scanned the young faces at the table. "That we could, and handed them out. The others I promised would have gifts by Christmas."

"That's only two weeks away. You sure you can raise the money to purchase more gifts?" Ryan asked.

"I'll help," Shandra said, feeling guilty for the gifts being ruined.

"That's sweet of you, but don't do it because you feel it was your fault." Colleen waved her fork around the table. "These people can all work their magic to get more dollars for the gifts that need purchased."

Her children and their spouses all groaned. Then collectively laughed.

"I have a feeling you get pulled into your mother's charity work quite often," she said.

"We do," Bridget said. "If we didn't love her, we'd consider it torture."

Everyone laughed and the conversation moved to the kids and what they'd asked Santa to bring them for Christmas.

As the evening wound down, Shandra took the interested family members out to the studio while Ryan entertained the rest.

Cathleen's older boys asked lots of questions. She herded the group back to the house and stopped at the back door, gazing out to the barn. The big lighted star she and Ryan had put on the end of the barn flickered. Power surges and outages were common this far out of town and up in the trees.

After the trip to the studio, the families started leaving.

She and Ryan stood at the front door waving as the car loads of Ryan's family drove down the road.

"Whew! That was fun but exhausting," she said, returning to the warm living room.

Ryan followed. He sat on the couch next to her. "It was a good distraction." He put an arm around her shoulders and picked up her hand with his free one. "Tell me what happened today."

She repeated the events and answered his questions about what each of the law enforcement people said and did.

"Damn, I wish I could help with this. They have to know by now that you aren't a suspect."

She held his hand over her heart. "I wish you were on this too, but it's not going to happen. I think Stu Whorter will do a good job." She had confidence in him but hadn't liked his partner. "Is he still working with that Pete guy?"

"No, I heard he moved." Ryan hugged her tight. "Stu's a good man. He'll get this solved."

"Yes, he will." But how soon? She didn't like being treated like a murder suspect.

Chapter Four

Shandra thrashed the whole night. Every dream involved Ryan. Ella, *Grandmother*, appeared in each one, peering down from a cloud, watching, as if on guard duty. What did that mean? Something was going to happen to Ryan?

She woke with a jolt and reached out for him. He was there. Warm and solid. The red numbers on the clock read 4:45. The alarm would go off in fifteen minutes. That was one of the downsides of where she lived. Ryan had to get up at five to get to work on time from here.

His warmth beckoned her. She snuggled up to him and dozed for fifteen more minutes dream free.

The alarm shrieked annoyingly. He hit the clock and rolled toward her.

"Morning."

"Hi." She wanted to ask him what he was doing today without sounding paranoid.

"This is the best part of the day," he said, wrapping his arms around her and pulling her close.

She curled into him, rubbing her cheek on the soft hair on his chest. "I agree." She'd never had this level of intimacy with a man before. This was what she'd yearned for and hadn't realized it existed. "Are you working that burglary today?"

"Yeah. Why?" He tipped her chin up and peered into her eyes.

"Just wondering. Think you'll learn anything about the guy from yesterday?" She couldn't bring herself to say body.

"Cathleen said she'd let me know what she hears through the dispatch office." He kissed her. "That's the best we can do until I hear there is forensic evidence. Then I'll pull in some favors."

"Sounds good. I'll be here working on my vase." She preferred not leaving the mountain after yesterday.

"I'll be back tonight." He kissed her again and swung his legs over the edge of the bed.

Sheba whined at the door.

"I'll feed her and let her out. You can keep sleeping." He walked out the bedroom door, shutting it behind him.

She slipped out of bed and dressed. After the dream she'd had, she wasn't going back to sleep.

Ryan returned. "I guess this means you're getting an early start on work."

"Yes. I'll fix your breakfast."

~*~

Ryan sat at his desk at the Weippe Sheriff's Office

in Warner, typing up the statements he'd collected from the homeowners of the break-in the day before. He'd planned to type them up last night, but after Shandra and Sheba found the body, he'd decided going home on time was a better option.

As he typed in the missing items, he wondered if there were any escaped convicts in the area. The list of stolen property sounded like someone going hunting or trying to stay out of sight. He finished the report and pulled up bulletins from the surrounding counties and states to see if someone was on the run.

His cell phone rang. Cathleen.

"Hello."

"There's talk around the office that the John Doe may have been a lawman." Her voice was quiet as she relayed the information.

"How did they come up with that?"

"They found a rental car. The name matches a name on the Deputy U.S. Marshal list. They requested a photo of him. Should be coming through soon." She muffled the phone. "Gotta go."

The line went silent. A Deputy U.S. Marshal? What would a Deputy Marshal be doing in Huckleberry?

He stared at the report for several minutes, not seeing the words, as his mind raced through all the reasons a Deputy Marshal would be in the area.

"You going to stare at that report all day, or send it to my desk?" Sheriff Wayne Oldham asked.

Ryan glanced up at his boss. "Just about finished."

"Heard about your girlfriend. You need some time off?" The sheriff had hopes of Ryan taking over his position when the man decided to retire. Because of that he tended to give him favors.

"No. She had nothing to do with what happened to the man. Just unfortunate that her dog ran into whatever was happening." Sheba seemed to have nothing wrong other than the cut. Which Chandler had stitched up nicely.

"Any leads on the theft at the Moulton's?" Oldham pulled up a chair and sat beside his desk.

"Not so far. I plan to check out campgrounds in the area."

"Why campgrounds?"

"Because of what was stolen. Camping gear, food, a hunting knife, and rifles." He nodded to the computer. "I'm also checking for fugitives. This feels like someone trying to keep a low profile."

"Sounds reasonable. Keep in contact with dispatch. If the person is hiding and has guns, best you don't let him know you're a cop." Sheriff Oldham stood. "Send that along and get out there looking."

"Yes, sir." Ryan finished the last of his report, saved it, and sent it to Oldham.

~*~

Ryan checked the two campgrounds between Warner and Huckleberry. They were heavily used in the summer but had few visitors in the winter. The first one didn't have any tracks in the snow leading into the campground. The second had one set of tracks. A truck by the width of the tracks. He idled through the ten inches of snow, following the tracks. A Chevy with a trailer on the back was parked by the restrooms. A ramp off the trailer and snowmobile tracks revealed whoever drove here was out enjoying the wintery forest.

He wrote down the license plate and hopped back

in his SUV. The satellite signal was sketchy at this spot. He pulled out his phone and called dispatch.

"Dispatch," announced his sister's voice.

"Greer. Cathleen, I need you to run down this plate." He rattled off the numbers and letters.

The sound of keys on a keyboard echoed in the phone as she brought up the information.

"William Arnold Perry. Forty-five-sixteen Fox Grove Lane, Warner. No warrants or arrests."

"I'm at South Tucker Campground and came across this vehicle with a trailer. It appears Perry is out enjoying a day of snowmobiling. I'm heading to Dry Flat next."

"Eleven-ten."

He swiped the screen on his phone and started up his pickup. Condensation had built up on the windshield from his conversation. Using his sleeve, he wiped at the inside of his window. A movement at the edge of the trees caught is attention.

There it was again. A flutter of color near the ground. He turned the vehicle off and trudged through the snow to the tree line. A male body sprawled across the snow. He was dressed in jeans and a flannel shirt. No boots. The wind picked up the tail end of the knit scarf around his neck, fluttering it in the air.

Ryan knelt by the body and dug into the back pocket, finding a wallet. The picture of the man stared back at him from the driver's license. William Arnold Perry. The body was frozen solid. The dark spot on his ribs was blood.

He pulled out his phone and called dispatch as he walked to his vehicle to get his crime scene pack.

"Dispatch," answered his sister.

"Greer. Cathleen, I found Perry. He's dead. Send search and rescue out here to follow the trail of his snowmobile. I'll start processing the scene."

"Eleven-twenty-four."

At Perry's truck, he tried the doors. They were all locked. Had the person who killed him only wanted the snowmobile or had he found the truck locked and took the next available vehicle?

Back at his SUV, he grabbed the handle on his pack and trudged back over to the body. He was still taking photos when the ambulance arrived. A deputy arrived after the ambulance and the coroner finally rolled in.

"When will Search and Rescue get here?" he asked Deputy Gerald Speaks.

"They should be about ten minutes behind me." Speaks scanned the area. "What do you need them for?"

"This man brought a snowmobile. It's missing." He walked over to the tracks he'd photographed. "There are three sets of prints. One when the victim rode into the forest, one when he came back, and a third when the killer drove off on the snowmobile." Ryan nodded to the forest. "I want you and Search and Rescue to follow the tracks. See where they lead."

"I'll get them on it when they arrive." Speaks strode along the now well-worn path in the snow back to the parking lot.

Ryan walked over to the coroner. "Any idea what killed him?"

"It appears to be a stabbing. The ME will be able to tell you more." Dr. Ram stood up. "As solid as he is, he must have been here overnight or longer."

"His name didn't pop up as a missing person when

I checked the license plate." It appeared he'd be asking the next of kin a few questions when he spoke with them.

"Can we take the body?" the EMT asked.

"Yes. Send it to Coeur d'Alene right away. This could be the second fatal stabbing in the same amount of days." He didn't like the idea of a maniac running around stabbing people.

The Search and Rescue team arrived. Speaks had them lined out.

Ryan climbed into his vehicle, started it, and blasted the heat onto his freezing feet. He pulled out his phone and called Stu Whorter.

"Whorter."

"Stu, this is Ryan Greer."

"I can't tell you anything about the case involving Miss Higheagle." Stu's tone said he wasn't going to take any butting in.

"We may have to talk about that case. I just found a snowmobiler at a camp site, stabbed in the chest. Is that anything like the body Shandra found?" He knew Stu was a stickler for protocol, but if their cases overlapped, he'd have to work with him.

"Yes. Where did you find the body?"

He told him about the body, the area, and that he had Search and Rescue following the snowmobile tracks.

"We'll know more when forensics come back," Stu said.

"Have you found out more about your body?"

"He is a Deputy U.S. Marshal. No one seems to know what he was doing in Huckleberry."

Ryan had an idea. "You might check out my

victim, William Arnold Perry. He could have been in witness protection and the marshal was coming to move him because his identity had been compromised."

"We'll look at all the angles. And I'll let you know what I learn from forensics." Whorter hung up.

Chapter Five

Shandra spent the morning refining the design for her next vase and wedging the clay she would use.

"You had a big party last night," Lil said, from over by the kiln where she was putting coasters in to fire.

"It was Ryan's family. I felt bad Sheba ran away with the presents when Mrs. Greer had put her reputation on the line for us." She'd had a good time last night visiting with Ryan's family. Although every time one of the women had her to themselves they'd asked when she and Ryan were getting married. A subject she and Ryan planned to leave hanging for a while. They both had their reasons to remain single.

"He's got a big one. You and him planning on tying the knot?"

She stared at Lil. It was the first time the woman

had ever linked them and not had distrust in her voice. "We've only briefly talked about it. What do you think?" While Lil had come with the ranch as a stray and took eccentric to a new level, she valued the woman's insights.

"I never had a chance to try the marriage thing. But me and Johnny were excited about the baby." She turned away.

Shandra didn't push her. The woman had been hiding the knowledge she'd lost a baby for decades. It wasn't until finding her lover's body in a clay bed that she'd learned the father of her baby hadn't left her on purpose.

Lil swiped her purple sleeved arm across her eyes and said, "That detective ain't my type, but he makes you happy. Bein' happy your whole life is a good thing." She stomped out the back door and left Shandra wondering about her words.

Pottery, Sheba, and her horses made her happy. Did she need a man? Memories of the last six months with Ryan in her life swamped her mind and her heart ached with happiness. She might be content with her art and animals, but having Ryan in her life made her happy and complete. Once they knew he was safe from gang retaliation, she'd ask him to marry her.

A grin tugged at her lips. That would surprise him. Her asking him. The idea settled warm in her chest. She continued wedging the clay, preparing it for her next vase. This one she planned to use a different technique than the others. The coil technique. She had plans to make it look like a pine needle basket.

The jazz tune "*Dream a little dream of me*" jingled in her back pocket. She pulled out her phone and saw

Ryan's name.

"Hello! I was just thinking of you."

"Good thoughts or bad?" he asked, his tone not as warm as usual.

"Good of course. What's wrong?"

"I found another body."

"Oh. That's not good."

"I'll be busy most of the day and night. Wondered if you wanted to meet me for dinner at Ruthie's about five. I'll need some cheering up after the day I'm going to have."

"I'd love to."

"Great. See you then." The line went silent.

She slipped the phone in her pocket and went back to work. Another body. Was the victim killed the same way? A shiver slithered up her back.

Her stomach growled but she had too much work to do if she wanted to get cleaned up and meet Ryan at Ruthie's. It would take her forty-five minutes to drive down the mountain and a half an hour to clean up.

~*~

Ryan drove into Warner and found 4516 Fox Grove Lane. The small house had a large metal building behind it. Cathleen had dug up everything she could find on the victim. He lived alone and was self-employed. The reason no one had listed him as missing.

He used the key he'd found in the man's pockets to let himself into the house. It was neat and tidy for a bachelor. A couple of photos of him and what appeared to be his parents. No photos of him and a female friend. Nothing in his house indicated that he might be in witness protection. He had all the usual photos, mail piled on the end of a small counter in the kitchen, and personal belongings in the drawer of the night stand.

If he wasn't linked to the Deputy Marshal could this have been a random killing? Ryan walked out the back door of the house and followed the muddy path to the large building behind. He unlocked the door and inhaled the aroma of fresh wood. From the mix of scents, the man had used many different varieties of wood for his projects. The benches were littered with pieces of wood in various shapes and sizes. On the side by the large roll up door stood a small enclosed trailer alongside of it were marks the right distance apart to be the space he'd parked the trailer used to haul his snowmobile.

There was nothing in the house or the shop that would have been a reason to kill the victim. He left the shop, locked it and the house, and climbed back into his SUV. While rummaging through the man's things, he'd found the phone number of the man's parents. This call was the one part of his job he'd never get used to or like.

~*~

Shandra stopped working at three and went in the house to change. She was anxious to learn what Ryan knew about the second victim. Her gut told her they were connected. She grabbed her purse and head to the door.

Sheba barked and loped to the door.

"Sorry girl, you should stay home and rest. When you get those stitches out you can ride shotgun."

The dog dropped her head and lay down on the cool tiles in front of the dead fireplace.

Her heart tugged at the dejected dog but it was best for her to stay home. Especially, if the killer was still hanging around Huckleberry.

She walked out the door and climbed into her warming copper-colored Jeep Wrangler. After having it shoved into a tree on the reservation during the summer, she'd worried about having to buy a new one. But the mechanics in Omak had put it back together and painted it, making the vehicle look like new.

Sheba stood at the large, great room window, watching her drive away from the buildings. The poor thing had to stay in the house to keep her stitches from getting wet. The dog loved to play in the snow. Soon her stitches would come out and she could play again.

And hopefully, they would soon get the person responsible for taking a life and attacking her dog.

~*~

Ryan was ten miles outside of Huckleberry when his phone rang.

"Greer," he answered.

"Vincent."

The voice and name sent him back ten years, to the day he was called into the captain's office and given the assignment to infiltrate the gangs on Chicago's west side.

"If you're calling me, it can't be good." Dread lodged in his gut like a bowling ball.

"I sent Deputy U.S. Marshal Clay Winston to warn you The Disciples know Shawn O'Grady didn't die and that he is living in Idaho."

Damn! The FBI agent he'd met in June had dug around and figured out where he'd seen him before. "I see. He hasn't contacted me."

"He's dead. I just heard he's the John Doe the Idaho State Police are trying to identify."

"That means there's a gang member or two here already." And he'd made a date with Shandra at Ruthie's.

"That would be my guess."

"Thanks for the warning."

"We can put you in protective custody and arrange for witness protection."

"I'm not going to live my whole life scared and running. I'll let the law enforcement I deal with know I'm a hunted man and see if I can't get free of this once and for all." Ryan killed the connection and pulled into Huckleberry. He parked a block down from Ruthie's and stared at the building. White lights twinkled in the windows. People were bustling along the sidewalks heading home or getting in some last minute shopping before the stores closed at six.

He'd put too many lives in danger walking into the café. And Shandra. He'd have to stay away from her until the person after him showed himself. The one thing he knew about the killer—he would take out anyone standing in his way of getting at Shawn O'Grady.

She'd understand. Ryan pulled out his phone and called Ruthie's. He left a message for Shandra, letting her know he wouldn't be joining her. Something came up, he'd call later.

Next stop would be the Huckleberry police and a conference call with the captain of the state police and his sheriff, explaining to them he was a target.

~*~

Shandra rolled down Huckleberry Street. She loved the Christmas season in the small ski resort. All the businesses glittered and glowed with silver, gold, red, and green. The street lamps were decorated with silver stars on top and Gingerbread men standing against the posts. Even the garbage bins in alleys were decorated like giant presents.

Embracing the spirit of the holiday, she walked into Ruthie's Diner and her spirits tumbled. She'd expected Ryan to be here waiting for her.

"Don't look so sad. He called and left you a message." Ruthie, owner and cook of Ruthie's Diner, slipped a piece of paper out of her apron pocket.

Shandra wondered what had come up since she'd talked to him and that he couldn't call and tell her rather than leave a note.

Her stomach grumbled. Half way to town her belly had started complaining it was hungry.

"Sit. I'm sure he had a good reason." Ruthie directed her to a corner booth and sat across from her. "Chandler told us about Sheba. How's our girl doing today?"

She stared into the concerned face of her friend. "She's fine. Wish I could say the same for myself. I can't believe another dead body was practically dropped at my feet."

"I know. Maxwell is thinking he should hang out with you for more business." The woman laughed. Maxwell Treat, her fiancé, was the son and business partner of the local mortician.

"I would rather they land at his feet than mine." Without looking at the menu Shandra said, "I'll have my usual."

Ruthie stood. "Bacon cheeseburger, sweet potato fries, and caramel shake, coming right up."

Shandra scanned the café. It was early for the huge

dinner crowd. An elderly couple sat in a booth across the café from where she sat. Two men sat on opposite ends of the counter. A younger couple sat in a booth near the door, and a middle-aged couple sat in a booth between the young couple and Shandra. The place wasn't hopping like it would be in an hour.

She flipped open the note and read.

Can't make it. Something came up. Call you later.

What could have come up? Maybe information about the body he'd found that morning. A shudder rippled through her. Two bodies in two days. This wasn't normal for the sleepy ski resort town.

Her gaze traveled around the room again. The elderly couple were getting ready to leave. She smiled at how the gentleman helped the woman with her coat and took her hand in his as he escorted her to the door. Sweet.

Movement at the counter drew her attention. The man wearing a baggy, black snowsuit, set his plate on a bill and walked out of the diner. His walk reminded her of a rapper she saw on a show. He kind of bobbed, bending his knees as he walked. She'd never witnessed anyone around here walk like that. He must have been a tourist up for the ski season.

Ruthie arrived with her shake. "This will ease the pain of eating alone." She winked.

Shandra laughed as her friend moved to the counter and started to clean up the plate and spot where the man in the snowsuit had sat.

"That thief!" Ruthie shook a bill at the door.

"What's wrong?" Shandra joined her friend at the counter.

"He only left a dollar for a six dollar meal."

"He wasn't a local, I'm pretty sure. I would have remembered his walk." She burned the image of his build and walk into her memory.

"I give people good food for their money and expect them to put the right amount down on a table when they walk out. It's robbery, that's what it is." The usually unflappable woman was getting angrier and angrier by the minute.

"Call the police station and have someone come take a statement. I'll tell them what I remember of him." She turned to the man on the opposite side of the counter. "Did you pay any attention to the man sitting here?"

"He was short, dyed red hair." The guy shrugged. "Didn't say much."

"Did he have an accent?" She wanted all the facts to tell whoever came to investigate.

"Didn't notice one. But he didn't say more than a word at a time." The man stood up and shoved a couple bills under the lip of his plate. "Thanks, Ruthie. Hope you catch the little twerp."

Ruthie was on the phone. "Yes. I want someone to come take down my theft report. I don't care if it's under the usual amount you do a report on. I want the thief caught, and I want my money." Her Kahlua colored skin glistened with perspiration and her lips pursed in annoyance.

"Ruthie, food's up!" called the backup cook.

Shandra slipped around the counter and picked up the food. It was hers anyway. "Thanks, Ben." She went back to her booth and ate the burger and fries, not enjoying the meal as much as she normally would.

Officer Blane barged into the diner. He scanned the

room, frowning when his gaze landed on her.

"I want to report a robbery," Ruthie said, cornering the young policeman.

Shandra shut their conversation out as she again contemplated why Ryan didn't show.

"Miss Higheagle."

The voice jolted her from her thoughts, causing her to drop her burger in the basket.

"Sorry, didn't know you were so far away."

She looked up at Officer Blane and his usual glaring eyes held sympathy. Why would he have sympathy for her? He'd only ever had animosity.

"Ruthie says you have some description of the man who didn't pay his bill." Blane had a pen poised over a notepad.

"Yes. I didn't really see his face. The other man at the counter said he had red dyed hair. He had on a black snowsuit that was too large for him and he walked like the rappers on T.V. You know, with a bounce in their step and their legs sort of bent."

"I know what you mean." He flipped the notepad shut and turned to leave. After two steps, he spun back around. "We'll all keep our eyes open for Detective Greer." He whipped around and strode out the door.

What did he mean by that? She shoved her food away and tossed a ten on the table.

Out in her Jeep, she pulled out her phone and dialed Ryan. It went straight to voicemail.

What was going on?

Chapter Six

Ryan sat in the Huckleberry Chief of Police's office staring at Marlow. He'd just finished his conference call with the state police captain, and Sheriff Oldham.

"I had a feeling you'd played in the big leagues while in Chicago, but I didn't have a notion you were wanted by the gangs." The sheriff leaned forward. "I'll have my men pull in anyone who looks suspicious and we'll run them through the Chicago gang task force list."

"I appreciate you keeping an eye out. But if the gang member sent to kill me has already killed twice, I don't think he'll come in peacefully to a police station." Ryan wasn't thinking of himself. He had a family and Shandra to protect.

"True. But we can keep an eye on him. We'll know soon enough if the two stabbings are related. Forensics should have your body by now and do a full autopsy."

"Yes. I have a favor to ask. Would you ask your men to keep an eye on Shandra Higheagle when she's in town? If the person asks around, he'll discover she's a way to get to me." His stomach clenched, thinking his past could bring Shandra harm.

"I'll tell the men." The chief tapped a pencil on the phone. "What about your family?"

"That's my next call." He stood.

Chief Marlow also stood, he held out his hand. "Good luck. We'll do what we can."

"Thanks, I appreciate that." Ryan shook hands and left the office. He was at a loss for where to spend the night. He couldn't go to Shandra's, couldn't go home, and wasn't going to put his parents or siblings at risk. If the killer was waiting for him at his place, he'd have to wait. He climbed into his truck and drove to one of the motels on the way to Huckleberry Ski Lodge. Changing motels each night would be how he'd live until they caught the gang member.

~*~

Shandra drove by the Huckleberry Police Station and caught the tail end of what she thought was Ryan's work SUV. She sped up and followed the vehicle. Why had he been in Huckleberry and not met her for dinner? And now it looked like he was going back to Warner.

No. He passed the highway turnoff. He was headed to the ski lodge. She was further surprised when he pulled into the first motel on the left. He went into the office, came back out, grabbed a bag out of his vehicle, walked to the very end of the building, and let himself into the room.

An hour passed with her watching the room. No

one approached the room. Was he working?

She pulled out her phone and dialed. It went straight to voicemail.

Something was wrong. Without thinking it through, she stepped out of the Jeep, grabbed the revolver under her car seat, shoved it into her purse, and walked up to the door where Ryan had disappeared.

She pressed her ear to the door and heard Ryan talking. Listening closer she decided he was having a phone conversation and was alone. She knocked on the door. His voice stopped.

"Ryan, I know you're in there—"

The door jerked open, his hand whipped out, caught the front of her coat, and pulled her into the room. He shoved the door closed and backed her up against it.

"What are you doing here?"

His tone and angry gaze had her swallowing a lump of fear that had lodged in her throat at his dragging her through the door.

"I saw you leave the police station and followed. I wanted to know why you were in Huckleberry but didn't show up for our dinner." The reason for her knocking on his door fired up her anger. "Why did you come here and not to my place? I've been watching. No one has come by, so it can't be for work."

"I had my reasons for staying away from you." He pulled her into his arms and kissed her. Then pressed her back against the door. "I have to stay away from you and my family. You need to leave."

She pushed against his chest and slipped out from under his grasp. His phone sat on the bed, his bag was on a chair by the door. "I'm not leaving until you tell me what is going on." She shed her coat and sat on the bed, placing her purse next to her.

He ran a hand through his hair, spiking it and giving him a devilish look. "I received a call today. The man you found in the sleigh was a Deputy U.S. Marshal sent here to warn me that a member of the Disciples gang was coming for me."

She gasped and her heart raced. "You think the member killed him and is after you?"

"That is a very strong possibility. It is highly unlikely in a place like this that the Deputy Marshal would run across an old nemesis." He sat down on the bed next to her. "You have to stay away from me. All he has to do is ask around town and connect you to me."

"Which is why I need to stay close to you. I'll be safer with you than at the mountain alone." She hoped between the two of them, they could stay vigilant and spot the person before he caught one of them.

He shook his head. "I can't have you or all of my family riding around with me. It would make his targets easier to get. I called my parents and siblings after I checked in here. I told them all to be watchful of unusual persons in their daily routines and to contact the sheriff's department or state police. I've filled all of them in on what is happening and why."

Shandra leaned her head on his shoulder. "None of this is your fault. You were doing your job."

He wrapped an arm around her shoulders. "I'd never be able to live with myself if anything happened to you or my family."

"Nothing will happen to us. You're a good cop. You'll find the person." And she'd remain open to Ella coming into her dreams tonight. They could use her sight to help them.

He kissed the top of her head. "If only I had the confidence in me that you have."

She leaned back and searched his eyes. "Can I stay the night? It would be safer than me driving back to my place?"

He laughed. "Leave it to you to use my own guilt against me. Yes."

"I'll call Lil and tell her I'm staying and to take care of Sheba." She dug into her purse and pulled the revolver out, placing the weapon on the bed.

"I see you were prepared to shoot me if you found me with another woman," Ryan joked.

She grinned. "That's a good idea, but no. I wanted to be prepared if I ran into a police sting or something."

"You thought there was a police sting going on and you still walked up to the door and knocked?" He shook his head and stood. "What am I going to do with you? You can't keep walking into danger. You aren't invincible."

"I know I'm not. I wasn't thinking about me. I was worried about you. It wasn't like you to leave a message with someone else and not call me." She was happy he was well and willing to let her spend the night with him, but she was still upset he didn't call her himself.

"I didn't want to answer all the questions I knew you would ask. When I left the message with Ruthie, I was sitting outside the diner worrying about all the people I could harm by walking in there. Not just you." He knelt in front of her. "I'd only received the phone call from Chicago minutes before. I still hadn't processed everything and I wasn't ready to be questioned."

She reached out and pulled his head to her chest. "I understand, now." She held him close for several minutes. "Don't ever shut me out. We're a team."

He turned his face up to hers. "I don't want you hurt."

"It hurts me more when you don't trust me." She released him. "I'll call Lil now."

Ryan rose from the floor and studied the strong woman he had in his life. When she'd called out from the other side of the door, he'd thought the gang member already had her and was using her for bait. His heart stopped beating as he peeked out the curtain and saw she was alone.

"I'll be staying in town with Ryan." She rolled her eyes and the corners crinkled as she smiled. "No, we aren't eloping. You're getting as bad as Ryan's family. I'll be home tomorrow. Thanks." Shandra ran a slender finger across her phone and gazed up at him. "Did you learn anything about the body you found today?"

He couldn't stop the grin or the shaking of his head. If they were together fifty years, he'd never understand her ability to bounce from topic to topic at the blink of an eye.

"I'll attend the autopsy tomorrow when the body has thawed out." He tugged off his shirt and stepped out of his pants, standing beside the bed in his boxers. "Let's get some sleep."

She held her booted foot out to him. "Give it a tug, please."

He grasped the heel of her fancy embroidered boot with both hands and worked it off her foot. She raised the other foot and he did the same.

"Mind if I borrow your toothbrush?" She walked over to his pack and dug through it, pulling out his toiletry bag.

"I guess not." He slipped into bed and listened. The traffic from the road going to the ski resort had lessened. He'd asked for the room farthest from the desk and asked the clerk to call his room if anyone came in asking for him. He was far from his vehicle but he could duck around the back of the motel and get to his rig while whoever looked for him was on their way to the room.

He glanced at Shandra's boots sitting next to his bag by the door. He shoved her revolver into her bag.

She returned from the bathroom and placed his toothbrush back in his pack.

"Put this and your clothes on the chair by the door." He handed over her purse.

Her gaze traveled over the items. "Quick get-a-way?"

"Yes."

Without a word, she slipped out of her jeans and sweater. Wearing her camisole and panties, she turned and placed her outer clothing on the chair with his. She slid under the covers and turned out the light.

~*~

Ella held up two fingers. "Do you mean two or peace, Grandmother?" Shandra asked standing in a cold white world. She spotted trees in the distance behind her grandmother. Ryan's SUV stood at the edge of the trees, the driver's side door stood open. "Is there two people after Ryan?" She took off running but could only walk due to the depth of the snow. "I have to warn him." She shoved her feet through the snow but the vehicle and trees seemed to get farther and farther away. "Help me! Help!"

"Wake up. Shandra, honey, you're having a dream." Ryan's voice penetrated her sleep.

Shandra's body shook. She was so cold. Shivers ran through her limbs.

"Hey, I'm here. You're safe." Warm arms wrapped around her.

She snuggled into the warmth and Ryan's woodsy scent. Several minutes passed and she started to warm up.

"What was your dream about?" he whispered next to her ear.

"Ella had two fingers raised. Your work vehicle was near some trees, the door was open. I tried to get to it but kept getting farther and farther away." She shivered remembering the sense of despair and cold.

His hand rubbed up and down her back. "Do you think the two meant there are two gang members out to get me?" His voice was soft against her ear, but his muscles tensed.

"I don't know. It could mean that. I fear it means you'll be lured to an isolated spot." She snuggled closer. "What time is it?"

"Three."

"Morning will be here soon."

He rolled her, holding his body over the top of her. "I won't let anything happen to you or me."

"I know."

His head lowered and she fell into the kiss, hoping to forget he was in danger for a while.

Chapter Seven

Ryan dressed while Shandra took a shower. He'd woke her at six to get her out of his room before too many people started moving about. Every time they were together, it gave the person out for revenge more chances to discover Shandra and use it against him.

She stepped out of the bathroom, her hair wrapped in a towel. "I don't suppose we can have breakfast at Ruthie's?"

He shook his head. "Not a good idea. I want you to go back to your place and stay there until I say you can come down."

This time she shook her head. "You know I can't do that. If you are in danger, I won't let you do this alone."

"I'm not. I have several police forces backing me up."

"I didn't see any outside last night." She put her hands on her hips and glared at him. "Knowing you, you told them to keep their distance so no one gets hurt." She shoved a finger into his chest. "What about you? You'll get hurt if you don't have someone looking out for you."

He'd never get tired of watching her when her temper flared. She was a beauty during any emotion but fury heightened her coloring and brought sparks to her golden eyes.

"I've had officers offer to ride along with me. I won't be alone." He tried to reassure her, but she only crossed her arms and tapped the toe of her fancy boot.

"Offered." She narrowed her eyes. "Did you take them up on their offer?"

He opened his mouth.

"No. I know you didn't. Or you would have gone to your house last night and not stayed in a motel."

She was too damn smart for her own good. But her tirade was taking some of the tenseness out of his muscles and making him see, he was being too stubborn about partnering up.

"I'll call and ask for someone to ride along with me." He pulled his phone out of the holder on his belt.

Her expression softened. "Thank you. I'll feel better knowing you have someone with you." She picked up her coat. "But I'd feel even better if that person was me."

He laughed and punched in Sheriff Oldham's number.

"Good to hear you laughing," Oldham said when he answered the phone.

"My girlfriend has that effect on me." Ryan ducked

as a pillow flew toward his head.

"I see. And why a call so early in the morning?"

"I would like to take you up on the offer of an officer riding along with me." He didn't like the idea of putting someone else in danger, but it might help him see his enemy sooner rather than too late. And if he didn't take a professional along, he knew Shandra well enough to realize she'd follow him, thinking she was keeping him safe.

"I can have Leeland drop by and pick you up."

"I'm still in Huckleberry. Thought it might be safer to stay away from my house."

"Good idea. I'll have him wait for you at the department. And keep your wits about you on the way here." The sheriff hung up.

Ryan put his phone away. "There. I'll have Captain Leeland riding with me." He pulled her into his arms. "I want you to go home and stay there. I'll call and give you updates, I promise." He knew if he didn't she'd be back checking up on him.

"Where are you going today?" she asked, hugging him around the middle.

"Checkout the autopsy, see if Search and Rescue came up with the snowmobile, and dig some more into the victim's life." He released her, picking up her purse and handing it to her. "Now go home."

"After a quick stop at the bakery." She kissed his cheek and opened the door. Snowflakes wafted in. "It looks like it snowed several inches and is still coming down."

"Drive careful going home." He walked up behind her and stared into the flurry of white falling from the sky. Did this start before the search and rescue found the snowmobile? He didn't like the fact the tracks could have been covered with the new snow.

Shandra pulled the hood of her coat up over her head and walked to her Jeep. She beeped the doors to unlock and climbed in.

He watched until she'd backed up and drove out onto the highway headed toward town. As upset as he was for her following him to the motel, he was glad they had last night. He could fool her, but he knew their chances of catching the gang member before he sought his revenge was slim.

~*~

Shandra had put on a happy face for Ryan but the dream had left a cold a lump of fear in her chest. She pulled into a parking spot across from the Daily Donut and crossed the street. Lil would have a fit if she didn't pick up the woman's favorite treat while it was fresh out of the oven.

It was early, not even seven yet and people occupied all the tables and chairs as well as made a line along one wall waiting to order. She dropped her hood and stood in line, studying the other patrons. Only half a dozen were locals. The others had to be skiers, getting their first burst of carbs and sugar before hitting the slopes.

The line slowly moved forward. She noticed a person in a dark snowsuit that was too big. He sat hunched over a table. His stocking cap rode low on his forehead and covered his ears. Almost as if he wanted to be invisible.

He glanced her way and she trained her attention on the couple next to him, but not before his eyes narrowed.

Knowing there was someone looking to kill Ryan, she found everyone sinister. She moved along with the line and forced herself not to look at the person in black again.

"Hey, Shandra. Haven't seen you around here this early before," Mark Surlee said, carrying a tray of fresh cinnamon twists out from the kitchen.

She sniffed appreciatively. "I don't usually come to town this early." She pointed to the twists. "I'll take six of those. Lil would skin me alive if I didn't bring her fresh cinnamon twists."

Mark laughed. "She buys some every time she comes to town." He leaned over the glass case. "I wouldn't want to get on her wrong side."

Shandra laughed. "Exactly!"

She paid the cashier and spotted the person in the black sloppy snowsuit walking out the door with the bounce of a rapper. He was the person who shorted Ruthie.

Shandra hurried to the door and looked up and down the street for the black snow suit. The streets were empty except for the few business owners opening their shops. The rapper as she was becoming to call him, was nowhere in sight.

~*~

Ryan swung by the sheriff's office and picked up Leeland.

"Where we headed?" the captain asked, clicking his seatbelt.

"To watch the autopsy on the snowmobiler." He put his work vehicle in gear and headed for the highway to Coeur d'Alene. With Leeland along, it gave him an excuse to not stop by his little sister's place. Bridgette would be mad, especially after he told his family to stay away from him until further notice, but it was the only thing he knew to do short of shipping them all to a tropical island until this all blew over.

"Oldham didn't tell me much about what's up." Leeland shifted slightly and watched him.

"Not much to tell. An enemy I made in Chicago is out to get me." He shrugged, but his gut was rejecting the two coffees and breakfast sandwich he'd eaten on the way to Warner.

"What's he look like? Kind of hard to keep my eyes peeled when I don't know what to look for."

He glanced over at his passenger. "I don't know what he looks like either. I have someone working on getting a name and description."

"That doesn't make sense. If he's an enemy you made, shouldn't you know who he is?" Leeland waved a hand, stirring up the aroma of bacon that must have clung to his clothes.

"I made an enemy of the Disciples gang. They discovered I'm still alive and have sent someone to finish me off."

Leeland whistled. "You pissed off the wrong people."

"Don't I know it." He didn't want to talk about his past. For the last eighteen months, he'd been thinking about a future. The rest of the way to the medical examiner's office, he directed the conversation to football. What little he knew of the teams came from catching sports radio newscasts. He rarely had time to watch a game.

Ryan pulled into the parking lot for the state forensic labs. "You going in?" he asked.

Yuletide Slaying

"Might as well." Leeland opened his door and stepped out.

Having promised Shandra he'd keep her posted, Ryan texted her that he was at the forensic lab. He stepped out of the SUV and locked the vehicle.

Leeland was already at the main entrance.

He caught up and passed the information counter. The text he'd received from Sheila Rickman, the ME doing the autopsy, said she would be in room four. Before entering the room, he pulled on plastic booties, a paper cover, and surgical mask.

"Right on time," Sheila said, as he stepped through the door.

The naked body of William Arnold Perry lay face up on the stainless table.

"We didn't find anything unusual about his clothing other than the tear from the stab wound and his own blood." Sheila probed the open wound on the victim's chest with her gloved finger. "I can tell you after consulting with the ME working on the victim from Huckleberry, the stab wounds are identical."

Ryan studied the woman's face. "You're saying the same person killed the Deputy Marshal that killed this man?"

"If not the same person, the same hunting knife." She picked up a scalpel. "We'll know if it was the same person when I get him open and see how far and how much damage was done internally."

His gaze blurred as he did mental gymnastics with all the information he had on both victims. No one had come up with any connection between the two. Until now. They were both killed with the same murder weapon. If the marshal was killed by the gang member looking for him, how did this victim play into the scenario?

"The left ventricle was punctured. The body cavity is full of blood." Sheila had the ribs forced open and had begun to pull out the organs.

"Is that the same as the other victim?" He had a sick feeling this man had been killed for his snowmobile.

"Yes. The wounds are inflicted from the same angle and punctured the same organ in both victims." She turned from the body. "I would say from the evidence gathered so far you have one person going around stabbing to kill."

He nodded and backed out of the room. In the hallway, he stripped off the sanitary clothing and headed to the front.

Leeland rose from the chair in the waiting room. "What did she say?"

"I'll tell you in the vehicle." He didn't need people panicking because there was a killer on the loose. One that it looked like would kill anyone in his act of revenge.

Chapter Eight

Shandra was relieved when she received Ryan's text saying he was at the forensic lab. He'd be safe while he was there. Or at least she wanted to believe that.

Lil had allowed Shandra one of the donuts before toting the sack off to her room in the barn. With Sheba sleeping under the table in the studio, she planned to work on her vase. It was a slow process of making perfectly shaped ropes of clay and adhering them together with water to form the shape of a water vessel used by her ancestors.

As she worked, the image of the man in the restaurant and donut shop swam in and out of her thoughts. She was positive he wasn't a local and his actions weren't those of a tourist or skier. Could he be the gang member sent to kill Ryan?

Stuck on the person in the baggy snowsuit, she washed her hands and wandered back to the house with Sheba following behind. Inside, she made a cup of hot chocolate and pulled out her phone. Ryan may not be happy with her for contacting him, but he had to know her suspicions.

~*~

Ryan parked his SUV in the ten inches of snow on the road leading into one of the more remote campgrounds between where he'd found the body of the snowmobiler and Huckleberry.

"What are we doing here?" Leeland asked, pulling on gloves and positioning sunglasses under his stocking cap.

"With both the victim at Huckleberry and the one I found being stabbed by the same person and the snowmobile missing, my guess is the murderer is staying either at a campground or in the woods between the two points." He settled his stocking cap on his head and tightened the strings on his gloves. "We'll hike into the campground and see what we find."

His phone beeped. He pulled it out and noticed Shandra had left a voice message. Judging by the bars on the phone he'd have trouble hearing the message. He shoved the phone back into his pocket and trudged through the knee-high snow, following the narrow road leading to the campground.

As they approached the area picnic tables with ten-inch white caps of snow, he noticed a tent set up under a trio of pine trees. While the tent was red and tan, it wouldn't be seen from the air with the large pine boughs crisscrossed above it. He didn't see a snowmobile, but planned to approach with caution.

Leeland motioned he'd go around to the other side of the camp. Ryan nodded and they both pulled out their Glocks anticipating a confrontation with a killer.

Steam puffed from his nose, fogging up his glasses. He shoved them up and was momentarily blinded by the sun and snow. Yanking the glasses back in place, he continued, stepping quietly through the knee-deep snow.

Closer inspection of the camp revealed the door of the tent open and flapping in the breeze. The snowmobile missing and the open tent, was a good sign the suspect wasn't here. He and Leeland met at the tent at the same time. It appeared an animal had gotten into the food supplies. The items he saw matched the list of items from the burglary four nights ago. He pulled out his phone and started taking photos.

"I think these are the items stolen from the burglary I'm working." He set up the folding camp stool to take a photo and spotted a hotrod magazine. "When was the last time you bought a magazine like that?" he asked Leeland.

"When I was in my twenties. Those dreams are gone after a mortgage and two kids." He picked up the magazine. A photo floated to the tent floor. Leeland picked it up. His face was sober as he turned the picture toward Ryan.

Sharp stabs of pain shocked his brain as he stared at a photo taken of him and two of the young men from the Disciples who hadn't made it out of the alley alive four years ago. He sat on the stool as the carnage and screams came back to him.

A hand on his shoulder squeezed. "I'll go back to the vehicle and get the crime scene pack and call it in."

He nodded, thankful Leeland took the photo with him. The memories of that night still haunted him when he was overtired and most vulnerable. Something had gone wrong that night. It was to be an easy bust, but somehow three gangs had converged on the alley behind the bar and tried to annihilate each other. The police arrived in time to clean up the mess and whisk him away to a hospital as far from the war as possible.

This was the temporary lair of the person out to kill him. He shook off the memories and scanned the area. There had to be a clue to who he was. Either he had been a member on the outer edges of the gang or he was new since he had a photo to use to find his victim.

He remained sitting on the stool, letting his gaze roam slowly around the inside of the tent. A small bulging pack in the corner caught his eye. It must not have had food or whatever animal had destroyed everything else would have torn the bag.

The size of the pack would look strange on him. As if he carried a child's pack. He snagged a strap and unzipped the main compartment. It held a pair of jeans, a T-shirt, boxers, and socks. He held the clothing up. They looked like a teenager's size and style. He swallowed. Please don't let it be a kid that was sent to kill me. The blood of any more young men on his hands was a burden he didn't want to carry with him.

He opened the smaller pouch on the side and found a comb, toothbrush, paste, and shampoo. No razor, which could mean he either had a beard or he was too young to shave.

The snow outside the tent crunched.

Ryan crouched beside the door and waited.

His crime scene pack shoved through the door

followed by Leeland.

"I got hold of dispatch on the radio and told them we have a possible location on the murder suspect and burglary." Leeland handed the pack to him.

"I don't like what I've turned up." He held up the clothing. "Looks like we have a young man trying to prove he's worthy of the Disciples and sent here to kill me as his initiation." He shoved the clothing back in the bag and handed it to Leeland who had on latex gloves. "Should get some DNA off the toothbrush in there."

He pulled off his winter gloves and dug in his pack for latex gloves. Leeland bagged the pack and tagged it while Ryan checked his notes on the burglary. While the Moultons hadn't given him a complete list, only camping equipment, the main items coincided with his list. All but a hunting rifle and knife.

"Do we wait here for him to come back?" Leeland asked, bagging the magazine and photo.

"It's the only clue we have, so yeah." He didn't like the idea of this person running around on a snowmobile. It gave him better mobility than if he had a car. He could hide out anywhere. A thought struck him.

He shoved out of the tent and walked around the campsite. There weren't any fuel cans. He had to be buying the fuel when he rode to, where ever he rode.

Leeland stepped out of the tent. "What are you looking for?"

"Fuel cans. We need to find out information on the victim's snowmobile. That will help us determine where the suspect is going." Ryan stared to the east. How far would Huckleberry be from here going across country? Or Warner? This campground was half way between both towns. With some farms in between where he could steal gas.

"We definitely need to find out all we can about the snowmobile and canvas the area to see if anyone has seen it." The county didn't have enough people to watch the camp and check for sightings of the man and snowmobile. He'd need the help of the state police.

"I'll wait here while you call and request back up." Ryan pointed to the evidence bags in Leeland's hands. "In fact, you should take those to forensics."

"I'm not leaving you here alone. If this is the suspect, he's killed two men already. And you are in his sights." He held up the bags. "Why don't you go lock these in the SUV and call for backup? I'll wait here."

Ryan didn't take the evidence bags. He didn't want to leave anyone here alone but if it had to be someone, it should be him. "Go ahead. I'll wait here."

Leeland shook his head. "I have seniority. I say you take this to the vehicle."

Ryan didn't like leaving a man who had a wife and two kids alone at the tent, but he was the higher-ranking officer. He trudged back through their previous tracks as quickly as he could. He placed the evidence bags in the back, and sat in the driver's seat. Steam had frozen on the windshield like a lacy picture frame. If Shandra were with him, she would pull out her sketch book and capture the look to put on a vase someday. Since she wasn't there, he pulled out his phone and took a picture.

He picked up the radio microphone.

"Greer."

"Dispatch," came the voice of Charles Wyland. He worked the opposite shift of his sister, Cathleen.

"Requesting two deputies come relieve Captain

Leeland and myself. We'll need twenty-four hour surveillance on this campsite until we apprehend the suspect." There was still a lot of investigating that needed to be done to catch the suspect.

"Ten-zero-six."

Ryan opened the door and heard a faint buzzing sound. There weren't any insects out in this weather. The sound grew louder.

It was a snowmobile.

Chapter Nine

The sound registered and he took off at a run toward the tent. He didn't want Leeland to encounter the suspect alone.

He broke out of the trees and spotted a dark blue snowmobile and someone in a black snowsuit with a dark colored helmet swerve away from the camp.

Leeland stepped out. "Stop! Police!"

The engine revved and both the man and machine disappeared among the trees.

"He knows we found him," Leeland said when Ryan stood beside him.

"He won't be back." Damn! They missed the chance to catch him. "Did he see you?"

"No. I heard the snowmobile coming and hid in the back corner of the tent." Leeland scanned the area. "He might have seen all of our footprints."

Yuletide Slaying

"Let's go. No sense staying here. He won't be back and if he does it will be a while. Our replacements will be here by then." Ryan trudged back to the SUV and cranked up the heater as they drove back to the county road.

~*~

Back in Warner, he took the pack and magazine, along with the photo to the forensic lab hoping either fingerprints or DNA would get them an identification of the suspect. After that he caught up with Stu Whorter of the State Police at a coffee shop.

"I understand our cases are connected," Stu said by way of a greeting.

"According to the ME." Ryan motioned to Leeland. "This is my body guard, Captain Leeland."

The two men laughed and shook hands.

"So you think the person who killed the marshal and the snowmobiler is out to kill you?"

He heard the reservation in Stu's tone.

Leeland jumped in. "The guy had a photo of Ryan in his possession. I think that makes it a pretty good assumption."

"I know you said that gangs in Chicago want you dead, but it seems extreme to kill two people before getting to you." He waved a hand encompassing the coffee shop. "It's not like you're a hermit and hard to get to."

That had him worried too. "I think he's going to go after my family before me. Gangs are like big dysfunctional families. He'll be saying, 'you killed my family, I'll kill yours.'"

"Do they know what's going on?" Stu asked.

"Yeah, I told them. But they are as pig-headed as I

am. They won't take a cruise or go anywhere safe."
He'd had the conversation with both his father and his
brother and neither one would budge and take their
wives some place safe. His brothers-in-law, on the other
hand, had packed up his sisters and nieces and nephews
and went to Disneyland.

"What about Shandra?" Stu asked, his gaze boring
into him.

"I can't shake her either." That reminded him,
she'd left a voice message. He pulled out his phone and
tapped the voicemail icon.

"*Ryan, I think the person you're looking for is in
Huckleberry. He stiffed Ruthie at the café yesterday and
I saw him in the donut shop this morning. He is short,
has on a baggy, black snow suit, wears a black stocking
cap down low, and walks like a rapper. I hope you're
staying safe.*"

He stood up to leave. If the person was in
Huckleberry and lurking, he'd overhear conversations
and could ask about him and Shandra.

"What's wrong?" Leeland also stood.

"That was a message from Shandra. She's seen the
suspect in Huckleberry. Twice."

Stu frowned. "How does she know he's the
suspect? She said she never saw him the other day."

"He stuck out to her. He didn't pay his bill at the
café and he was at the donut shop this morning. She
says he's short and has on a black, baggy snowsuit."

"The guy on the snowmobile had on a black
snowsuit," Leeland added.

"She said he's short. That fits with the clothes we
found. And he walks like a rapper." This one he had no
clue what she meant.

"Rapper?" Stu studied him like he'd uttered a language he didn't understand.

"Rapper. Like Eminem. Snoop-dog." Leeland held his hands palm up. "I have teenage kids."

Ryan shook his head. "Okay. How do they walk?"

Leeland walked to the door and back, his knees bent slightly and his body bobbed with each step. "You know swagger and bounce."

Ryan and Stu laughed and shook their heads.

"We have a bit of a description. We'll swing by my victim's place and find information on his snowmobile, then head to Huckleberry and look for a rapper in a baggy, black snowsuit." Ryan hoped they had this guy apprehended by the end of the day. He didn't like the idea the suspect could be gathering information on his family and Shandra.

~*~

Shandra couldn't stay focused. She hadn't heard back from her message to Ryan hours ago. Her stomach rumbled. She'd forgotten to eat lunch.

"Come on, Sheba, let's get something to eat."

Lil stepped out of the barn as she exited the studio.

"Any chance you plan to go back to town today?" Lil asked, her hands covered in a white substance. When she walked closer, the menthol scent gave away the substance on her hands. The liniment Lil used on her old horse.

"I hadn't planned to, but I could go if you need something." She noted the worry lines wrinkling the other woman's brow.

"I don't want to leave Sunshine. She's had a horrible time getting around today." Tears glistened in Lil's eyes. "I don't think she's going to make it through this winter."

Shandra put an arm around the shorter woman's shoulders. "You stay here. I'll go get the liniment. Sunshine will be comforted by you."

"Thank you." Lil rolled out of her one-armed embrace and strode back into the barn.

It looked like she'd be in town for dinner. Shandra entered the house, changed out of her work clothes, and picked up an apple to tide her over until she could sit down to a decent meal.

Her phone jingled a jazz tune. Hoping to see Ryan's name, she was surprised to see Naomi, her close friend and owner of one of the galleries in town.

"Hi, Naomi," she answered.

"Hey, Shandra. Any chance you'll be coming into town the next couple of days?" Naomi talked soft and slow. She was the complete opposite of Ted, her constantly in motion husband.

"I'm headed that way right now. Lil needs more liniment for Sunshine. Why?" She stepped into her boots.

"A man came in today specifically to look at your work. He was admiring your piece up at the lodge and Meredith Gamble told him you had pieces for sale at our gallery." The excitement in Naomi's voice made her think they'd sold a piece.

She could use the money with the holidays coming up. It would be the first one that she and Ryan spent as a couple. "Which piece did he buy?"

"None, yet. He really likes the work but said he prefers to meet the artist when he can. He said that helps him make his decision about buying." Naomi sighed. "He's very good looking. You'll want to meet him. How about meeting us at Rigatoni's about six?"

She had planned to dine in Huckleberry but had hoped it would be with Ryan. "I can do that. I'm headed in now and have to purchase the liniment first. See you at six." She disconnected the call and pulled her coat on.

Sheba stood by the door, her tail swinging in anticipation of a ride.

"Why not. I could use the company. Come on." They walked out to the barn. She opened the big doors and started the Jeep. Sheba took her usual place in the back seat, her tail wagging so much she created a breeze in the front seat.

Shandra stepped out of the Jeep to close the barn doors.

"I'll get them," Lil said, walking out of the barn, wiping her hands on a towel.

"Thanks! I left the lights on. I'm having dinner with Naomi and Ted and might be late." She hadn't had dinner with her two friends in a while. Hopefully, the buyer wouldn't spend the whole evening with them.

"I'll make sure the barn lights are on when you come in."

Shandra closed the door and drove down the narrow path between the trees she called her lane. Once on the county road, she picked up speed and was in Huckleberry in less than an hour.

Her stomach growled again, unappeased by the apple. She drove to the feed store first to get the liniment.

Harvey and Louise, the owners of the feed store, greeted her and Sheba. Harvey headed to the back of the store.

"Oh my! What happened to you, beautiful?" Louise asked as she touched the bandage around the dog's neck.

"She had a cut that needed stitches." Shandra walked over to the shelf with the liniment. To avoid having another emergency where they ran out, she grabbed two jars.

"Oh no! If you're buying two jars, Lil's horse must not be doing well." Louise rang up the price of the jars.

Sheba walked over with a stuffed squirrel in her mouth.

"I guess we're buying that too." Shandra patted her dog's head.

Louise laughed and rang up the price of the toy. "She knows where the toys are. Maybe we should move them so you don't have to buy one every time you come in."

"It will give her some company while I have dinner with Ted and Naomi." Shandra picked up the bag of liniment. "Thanks."

Harvey walked in from the back of the store grumbling.

"What's wrong?" Shandra asked. She'd never seen the man upset about anything.

"Some yayhoo on a snowmobile syphoned the gas out of our forklift at the back dock." Harvey smacked his hat on the counter. "I just filled it up this morning. It wouldn't start so I could put it in for the night and I saw the tracks and the dribble of fuel on the side of the lift."

"Call the police. Maybe they can find the person." Shandra had a gut feeling she knew who had stolen the fuel.

Louise shook her head. "First that person running

out and not paying his bill at Ruthie's, and Oscar catching someone digging through the donations left in the church entry. What's happening to our nice little town?"

"Call the police," Shandra said to the couple and headed to her Jeep. As soon as the Jeep was running and the heat blasting, she pulled out her phone. She needed to know Ryan was okay.

Chapter Ten

Ryan sat at a computer in the Huckleberry Police Station typing up the events of the day. Leeland had taken the SUV back to Warner with orders for Ryan not to leave the police station until he returned for him in the morning. He wasn't looking forward to sleeping on the cot in the back room, but he'd slept there before. His other alternative was to call Shandra, but he planned to stay away from her until they caught the person hunting him.

His phone buzzed.

Shandra.

He slid his finger across the screen. "Hello, beautiful."

"I've been worried about you. Did you learn anything new?" Her husky voice always eased the tension brought on by work.

"It's been a frustrating day." He stood and walked down the hall to the room with the cot where he'd be sleeping and shut the door. Hazel was on dispatch tonight, and she had a penchant for eavesdropping.

"Why was it frustrating?" Her tone reflected interest and concern.

"We found the camp where the person who stole the snowmobile was staying." He didn't want to worry her, but she needed to know of the danger that was so close. "We found clothing for a small-sized person, all the camping, hunting gear that had been stolen…" He took a breath. "And a photo of me with a couple of the gang members."

She gasped. "So he is the person looking for you?"

"It appears so."

"He stole gas from the forklift at the feed store." Her tone was all business.

When it came to righting wrongs and solving murders, he'd prefer her on his team any day.

"How do you know it was him? Did someone see him?"

"No. But Harvey said there were snowmobile tracks up beside the forklift and he could see where the fuel had dripped while it was being syphoned." She paused. "I'm in town picking up liniment for Sunshine and having dinner with Naomi and Ted. You want to join us?"

He did want to see her, but he'd put her in danger if he did. "I can't. I have all the reports to write up tonight. And I don't want this person to see us together. I want you safe." His voice dropped before he caught it. She knew how he felt about her, but he didn't want her thinking because he could be killed any minute that he wanted her to say three words she'd yet to say.

"I understand, but that doesn't mean I won't be wishing you were there the whole time." She inhaled. "Are you in Warner? I could drive over after dinner…"

He'd love to hold her tonight… "No. I'm not in Warner. I'm spending the night at the Huckleberry Police Station. Leeland's orders."

"I see. You want Sheba and I to come by and cheer you up after dinner?"

A laugh burst out before he could stop it. "You and Sheba? That would get Hazel in a twitter."

"Or, I could drive down the alley and you could hop in and we'd take you to the ranch."

It was so tempting. The bed they shared at her ranch was much more comfortable than the cot. But did he dare risk her life to make himself comfortable? "I think it's best you have your dinner and go home. The less time you spend with me the better."

"If you change your mind, text me." The disappointment in her voice would have had him jumping for joy any other time. Right now it only tugged harder on his heart.

"I won't change my mind. You text me when you're home safe."

"I will. Good night." She ended the call.

It was for the best. If he'd kept talking to her, he would have weakened and put her at risk. He left the room, hoping they found this guy and took away the threat.

~*~

Shandra shoved her phone in her purse. Tears burned behind her eyes. She knew why Ryan was keeping his distance. But it hurt knowing he had to be experiencing all kinds of emotions and she wasn't there to help him. Sheba rested her head on Shandra's shoulder.

"Thanks, girl. I needed a hug." She held the slobbery chin on her shoulder a minute, soaking in her dog's caring soul. "I'm better now, thanks." She patted the furry face, and Sheba sat down in the back seat.

Shandra put the Jeep in drive and headed down the road, parking in front of Dimensions Gallery, the one Ted and Naomi owned. Their store was only two blocks from the restaurant. She'd walk now and could walk back with them after the meal. Glancing at the clock on the dash she was running late.

"Sheba, you be good. Your fur coat will keep you warm and you have your new toy to keep you company. I'll bring you back a steak bone." Shandra patted the wide black head and kissed her ear. "Be good."

Out of the vehicle, she locked the doors and headed down the sidewalk toward Rigatoni's. The streets were lined with white Christmas lights and the stores had left the Christmas displays lit up in the businesses. She wished she wasn't in a hurry and could enjoy the holiday atmosphere.

Miranda Aducci, the daughter of the restaurant owners, met her at the door. "Ted and Naomi were starting to get worried about you." She hugged Shandra. "You're never late, and you don't want to miss the hunky guy with them." The young woman fanned her face. "He is hot stuff."

Shandra laughed. "Well, I'll find out if he's single and then tell him about how wonderful you are."

Her big brown eyes grew rounder. "You'd do that for me?" Miranda had a beautiful face, stood over six foot, had a robust build, and a robust personality. It would take a man who was very confident to handle being by her side.

"Yes, I would do that for any friend. And I consider you a friend." Shandra shed her coat.

Customers walked through the door.

"Which way?" she asked, waving Miranda away to help the newcomers.

"The circular seat facing the mountain."

She should have known Naomi would pick that seat. It was the best one in the restaurant and would impress the buyer.

Walking past other tables, she recognized an older couple who frequented Ruthie's and were not usually here in the winter. She finger waved to them and continued on.

Naomi half stood and waved as she rounded the corner.

Shandra waved back and hurried over. "Sorry, I'm late. It took longer to get the liniment than I thought it would. Her cheeks heated not telling her friends the truth. But she wouldn't talk about Ryan's concerns in front of a stranger and because Ryan didn't want anyone other than law enforcement to know about the man out to kill him, she would never share that, even with Naomi.

Naomi grinned. "I bet you were talking to Ryan."

She glanced at the man on the other side of Ted. He was drop dead gorgeous, but when he smiled his eyes didn't hold any mirth.

"You caught me. Yes, I was talking to Ryan. He's been so busy lately we haven't seen much of each other." She slid onto the bench seat next to Naomi. Her friend hugged her around the shoulders.

Ted held out his hand and grasped hers, giving it a squeeze. "Good to see you." He released her hand and motioned to the man beside him. "Shandra Higheagle, this is Mick Sterling. He fell in love with your vase at the Lodge and came into the gallery today looking for more of your work."

She extended her hand over the table. "Mr. Sterling."

"Mick. Everyone calls me Mick." His grasp was strong. He held her hand and turned it over. "You have rough hands for a woman."

The comment came from nearly every man she encountered. "It's because I work with clay which dries my hands out and the abrasiveness wears on the skin."

He smiled. This time a small light shone in their deep blue depths. "You were so lovely when you first walked in, I thought maybe these two had hired a beautiful woman to represent you and sway me to buy."

"We would never do that," Ted said, sliding closer to his wife, his face turning crimson.

"I apologize. In my circles, it isn't unusual for someone trying to get my business to play tricks." Mick released her hand.

"That must make knowing who is truthful and who isn't hard." Shandra wondered at his business that people would try to swindle him.

"It is. That is why I always want to see the artist when I purchase new artwork. I've been scammed twice where I thought I was purchasing an original from a new artist and discovered it was a knockoff of someone dead." His gaze locked onto hers. "Your friends tell me you dig the clay you use from

Huckleberry Mountain."

"Yes—"

"Sorry to interrupt." Miranda stood by the table. "If I can get your orders, they will go in before a large group that arrived after you."

"That's so thoughtful, Miranda." Shandra smiled at her friend. "I'll have my usual, with an appetizer, I'm starving. I was working today and didn't eat lunch."

"I'll have whatever Shandra is having," Mick said.

"You want the steak bone to go as well?" Miranda joked.

Mick looked stunned and the table laughed.

"I have a large dog who loves when I come here and bring her back a bone," Shandra said enlightening him.

He laughed. "No bone for me."

Naomi and Ted ordered. Miranda left but not before sending a bright smile Mick's direction.

"You actually miss meals to work on your art?" Mick leaned forward, his forearms on the table.

"She's known to go without sleep if an idea comes to her," Naomi said, picking up her water and taking a sip.

"Really? You work all night? I can't imagine a potter working all night."

"Why not? When you have a business deal…What do you do for work?" Shandra was curious about his money. He had on an expensive sweater, and the one shoe she'd seen when she walked up to the table had looked expensive.

"I import and export collectibles. That's why I know a work of art when I see it." He winked. But the action felt forced.

She'd become skeptical of people with money who couldn't give a definite answer to what they did. Her stepfather had had a couple of friends that she was sure dealt in illegal activities. They'd always been hard to pin down what they did for a living.

"I'm not here to talk about me. I want to learn about the process you go through to make a vase."

"You should go to her studio and see the whole process," Naomi chimed in.

Any other time she would have been more than happy to give him a look into her world. Right now, with someone out to kill Ryan and her possibly a target as well, she didn't need extra people at the ranch.

"Right now isn't a good idea. I'm right in the middle of a project. One that is different from the usual. I'm not ready for anyone to see the technique."

"I won't look at what you're working on." He crossed his heart. "I promise."

She shook her head.

"What would it hurt? Ted or I could bring him out tomorrow," Naomi said, smiling at Mick and looking at her husband for acceptance.

"I could spare half a day tomorrow," Ted said.

"Half a day?" Mick said.

"I live an hour from town. It would be two hours just traveling." She hoped he didn't have the time to spend. It would be rude to outright tell him 'no' when he could be a client who would purchase multiple pieces from her. She had several clients who followed what she had out in galleries and purchased the pieces they liked.

He frowned. "I'll have to check my schedule when I get back to the lodge and see if I can take half a day to see your studio."

Miranda arrived with their soups and salads. She managed to brush up against Mick. His eyes opened wide and he checked her out.

Shandra didn't want her friend to have a short fling with this man. She didn't trust him and he was only here on vacation. But she knew how hard it was for Miranda to find a man.

"Mick. Are you vacationing with anyone?" she asked, while Miranda was still within hearing.

"No. I decided at the last minute I wanted to take some time off from work and enjoy a ski vacation." He picked up his wine glass. "Could you bring us another bottle of this wine, please." His eyes sparkled at Miranda as he asked her.

Shandra couldn't miss the way Miranda's cheeks darkened.

"Yes, sir." She hustled away, leaving Shandra wondering how desperate her friend must be to come on so strong with this stranger. And she didn't care for the glint of speculation in Mick's eyes.

Chapter Eleven

Ryan finished the reports around ten. He stood and stretched.

"Want some coffee?" Hazel asked, sitting at the dispatch desk knitting.

"No. That would just keep me awake. Think I'll go take a quick shower and go to sleep." He grabbed his coat from the back of the desk chair.

"Ok. I know why Leeland told you to stay here." Her faded green eyes widened behind her glasses. "I hope this one person is the only one after you. It would be a shame for you to have to spend your whole life worrying someone is after you."

That was the one thing he didn't know. If they did stop the first person sent, would another and another be sent until his name showed up in the obituaries of the Warner Tribune?

"Your guess is as good as mine. My hope is this person was sent by the gang but is a family member of someone who died. Once he fails I would think that would be the end of it." He shrugged. "I just hate that it puts everyone I encounter at risk until we get him." Nodding to the door. "It wouldn't hurt to keep that locked tonight."

Hazel stood. "Good idea. Russ won't be back for a couple hours. He's out driving around looking for the snowmobile now that we have a description." She walked to the door and locked it. "Go take that shower and get some rest."

"Thanks." He headed to the back room. Dumped his coat on the cot and picked up his pack with his clothes and toiletries. He glanced at his phone. No text from Shandra. It was only a little after ten. She could still be driving home. He headed to the small shower stall in the men's restroom.

~*~

Shandra left Rigatoni's with Naomi and Ted. She didn't want to remain alone with Mick. The more wine he drank the more his gaze wandered lower than her face and his hand strayed to Miranda's hips. She used the excuse of wanting to talk business with them. She'd wanted to warn Miranda to take it slow with Mick, but she'd been busy with another table when Naomi decided it was time to leave.

They admired the decorations as they walked to the Jeep and store. The couple lived in the apartment over the store.

"Why were you against Mick coming to your studio?" Ted asked when they stopped beside her Jeep.

"I do have a new project that is different and

technically hard. It requires lots of concentration. I would hate to have something happen to it and have to start over." She hugged Naomi. "But if he insists on coming out before buying a piece, I'll figure out something. Just give me a warning you're coming."

"You know I would never show up uninvited. I wouldn't want Crazy Lil to shoot me." Ted used the moniker the town had for Lil. Because the eccentric woman dressed in purple, had been known to pull a gun on someone showing up at the ranch unannounced, and refused to leave the ranch after her grandparents' death no matter how many people had lived there since, they'd dubbed her crazy.

"I like that Lil keeps an eye on things. Especially when I'm gone." Shandra unlocked the vehicle and slid in. The windows were all frosted on the inside from Sheba's breath.

"You want to come in for a cup of tea while your windows defrost?" Naomi asked.

"If you don't mind me bringing in the cause of all the inside frost on my windows."

Sheba whined and pushed between the front seats.

"You know we love your big mutt. Come on, Sheba," Naomi said.

Shandra slid back out, leaving the vehicle running. Sheba jumped out behind her and nudged Naomi with her muzzle.

"Yes, I have a biscuit for you. Come on."

The locks clicked and Shandra followed her dog and friends into the gallery. Ted locked the front door behind them. The lights shining on several of the pieces throughout the gallery lit their way to the backroom. This room was where they crated and uncrated art and housed the stairs to the apartment above.

When they were all snug in the small kitchen drinking tea, Naomi looked her in the eyes. "What is up with you and Ryan?" She put her hand up. "Don't say nothing. I saw you and his family together before the parade. It looks to me like things are getting serious."

She should have known her friend would want to know what was happening. "Honestly? We are closer and have mentioned the M word. But at this moment, things are up in the air. I can't tell you why. You're better off not knowing. The only thing I do know, is having to keep my distance from Ryan has made me realize how important he has become." She shrugged and felt the tears burning behind her eyes. Crying in front of her friends wasn't an option. She turned to Sheba sitting beside her chair. "Think those windows are thawed?"

"Woof!"

"I guess we'll be going. Thanks for the tea." Shandra stood.

Naomi put a hand on her arm. "You're not getting away that easy. You better tell that man how you feel or you'll lose him. And does any of this not seeing each other have to do with the body Sheba scooped up in the sleigh full of presents?"

She stared at her friend. Only Naomi would follow up something emotional with a packed question.

"Yes and no. I can't talk about it."

Naomi narrowed her eyes and studied her. "Do they think you did it? And you have to stay away from Ryan because you're a suspect?"

"No. I'm not a suspect. They aren't letting him work the case because I found the body. He's busy with a robbery and the other body."

"What other body?" Ted jumped into the conversation.

Great! This was exactly what the law enforcement community was trying to keep from happening by not mentioning Ryan had a killer after him. Panic.

"A snowmobiler."

"Oh, yes we heard about that. But that was over at South Tucker. I thought you meant here in Huckleberry." Ted leaned back and sipped his tea.

Shandra refrained from mentioning snowmobiles could cut across country that was only thirty miles away. If they knew the two murders were connected Ted wouldn't be so cool. She pulled on her coat, and Ted stood to escort her to the front door.

At the door Ted stopped her before she walked out. "You know she isn't going to give up until you are happily married."

A laugh escaped her. "Yes. Your wife believes I should be as happily married as you two."

He grinned. "You deserve a good man."

She walked out to the still running Jeep, with clear windows and unlocked the doors. Sheba hopped in the back door when she opened it.

A shiver slithered up her back. She looked up and down the street and only saw a couple leaving Rigatoni's. Why am I so nervous? She slid into the driver's seat and locked the doors before driving off.

Shandra was glad for Sheba's company on the ride home. The dog bumped her and made noises, keeping her awake. She rehashed the way Miranda and Mick seemed to be getting friendly. Miranda was a smart young woman. But too naïve to dally with the likes of

Mick Sterling, of that she was positive. Tomorrow, she'd call the restaurant and have a visit with the woman.

The welcoming glimmer of the white lights she and Ryan had hung from the barn roof, studio roof, and front of the house, made her smile. She couldn't wait for Christmas Eve when she and Ryan would hike into the forest and come back with the perfect Christmas tree. She parked the Jeep and slipped out to open the barn doors. She hadn't seen any sense in building a garage when so much space in the barn went unused.

Sheba bailed out of the Jeep and headed to the corner of the barn.

"Don't take off. I'll be going right in the house," she said to the dog, who squatted and did her business.

Shandra drove the Jeep into the lit barn. Once inside, she slid out of the vehicle and flipped the lights off. The big barn doors swung easily on well-oiled hinges. She dropped the large wooden board into place and turned to the house. Her limbs froze as a shadow moved in the dim light of the great room.

Ryan was at the station. Lil would be in the barn.

Sheba bounded out from the back of the barn and started for the house.

"Sheba! Come!" she whispered loudly.

The large furry dog sat on her haunches and looked back over her shoulder.

"Come!" she whispered again and headed down the side of the barn to the back door that opened next to the tack room—the only room Lil would live in.

Sheba breathed heavily behind her, as Shandra reached for the barn door latch.

Once they were both inside the barn, she felt her

way to the door to Lil's room.

She knocked.

No one answered.

She knocked louder.

Still no answer.

She opened the door. "Lil. It's me Shandra."

Nothing.

Running her hand up and down the wall, she searched for the light switch. Found, she flicked it on. The room was empty except for Lewis, Lil's orange cat.

There hadn't been any lights in the stalls, so she couldn't have been in a stall with Sunshine. Which reminded her of the liniment in the Jeep. Lil had to be in the house. But why? She only went in there to clean or when she was invited.

She flicked the light off and turned on the overhead light in the barn. Sheba ran to the big double doors Shandra had opened to get the Jeep inside. The dog whined and scratched at the ground.

"Just a minute. I'll get the liniment and we'll go to the house."

The doors rattled and Sheba growled.

Chapter Twelve

Ryan glanced at his watch again. Why hadn't Shandra text him? It was after eleven. She should have been home by now. Unable to sleep not knowing what was happening to her, he decided to check on her.

Are you home? He text.

Five minutes went by without a response. That wasn't like her. She would have remembered to text him when she arrived home.

He pulled on his pants and headed barefoot out to the dispatch area.

Hazel's eyebrows rose at his bare feet and T-shirt. "Can't sleep?"

"I haven't heard from Shandra. She was in town having dinner with Ted and Naomi. She was supposed to text when she arrived home." He squinted to see out the windows. "Has it snowed or is the county road out her way obstructed?" Even as he asked he knew she would have let him know if she'd stayed in town.

"Weather hasn't changed since this afternoon and nothing has happened on county road fifteen. You try calling her?"

"I text and she didn't respond." He pulled his phone out of his pants pocket. Pressing her photo on his phone, he held the device to his ear and listened as it rang.

He headed to the back room to finish dressing, when a breathless voice said, "Hello?"

"Shandra? Are you all right?" His heart thudded hard against his chest.

"Yes. No," she whispered. "I'm in the barn. I started to the house and saw a shadow in the great room. So I came back in the barn to get Lil but she's not in her room." She drew in a deep breath. "I thought she might be in the house, but someone or something just banged on the doors and Sheba growled when she sniffed under the door."

Fear for her, sent blood whooshing in his ears. He was a good half hour away. But he calmed his voice as he said, "Could it have been wind that hit the doors? If no one tried to open them that would make sense. But lock yourself in the Jeep, hang up from talking to me, and call the house and see if Lil answers." It was a long shot, but given they knew someone wanted to cause him harm and could very well want to start by taking away the people he loved, he wanted Shandra to be extra careful.

"Okay. I'm in the Jeep. I promise I'll call you right back."

The phone went dead. He pulled on his socks and

boots and had his coat on when his phone buzzed.

Shandra.

"Is it Lil in the house?" he asked.

"Yes. She was warming blankets in the drier to put on Sunshine to keep her warm. It must have been the wind that blew on the doors. I'm going into the house now."

The sound of a car door revealed she was out of the Jeep. He was glad she was keeping him on the phone.

"Why are you getting home so late?" he asked to keep her talking.

"Naomi and Ted brought a prospective client to dinner. Then they had me up for tea while the windows defrosted on my Jeep."

He heard the crunch of snow under her feet and the click of the backdoor latch.

"Lock the doors now that you're in the house." He didn't want anyone sneaking in that didn't belong.

"I did. Are you safe?"

"Yes. I'm in the back room of the station." He slipped out of his coat and slowly unlaced his boots. "Promise me you'll stay put until this is over."

"I can't. We don't know how long it could take."

He had to agree with her comment. "Then stay away from strangers. We don't know yet what this guy looks like."

"I will. And if it's the same little man I've been seeing, I know what he looks like. Well, how he's dressed and how he walks."

"Stay out of the woods. If he's running around on a snowmobile he could be anywhere." He wished he could be holed up at the ranch with her, but it wasn't realistic. He had two cases to work and needed to keep distance between them.

"I will. You be careful too." She yawned. "I'm going to bed now."

"Sleep tight." His voice dropped again, giving away the emotions he couldn't seem to control.

"I'll try, but it's hard when you aren't here." Her self-conscience laugh tugged at his heart. "I didn't mean to sound like a clingy woman."

"Not at all. With my life in jeopardy there are many things I want to say to you." He stopped. Playing on her sympathy wasn't the way he wanted to get her acceptance of a marriage proposal.

"I know. But saying them makes it feel like…like justice won't prevail."

He knew exactly what she meant. "Yeah. Like that."

"Good night." The connection cut off.

He set the phone on the table next to the cot, turned out the light, and stripped down to his shorts and T-shirt. Even as tired as he was, sleep didn't come quickly enough to keep him from thinking all kinds of frightening scenarios.

~*~

Shandra put her phone in the bedroom by her bed and walked back out into the great room. Lil sat on the couch reading a magazine as the drier down the hall thumped.

"Do you plan to come in here all night long and heat up blankets for Sunshine?" She sat on the opposite end of the couch.

Sheba lay sprawled out in front of the gas fireplace.

"I plan to get them hot enough they'll stay warm underneath a sleeping bag I'll toss over the top of the blankets and Sunshine." Lil glanced up from the magazine. "I'll go to town tomorrow and buy a heated blanket for her at night."

"That's a good idea. I had an electric blanket as a child but I don't own one now." She studied the older woman. "Don't you have one, sleeping out there in the barn in the winter?"

"Nope. With Lewis and my down sleeping bag, I stay warm and toasty."

The drier buzzer vibrated the air.

"I'll be out of your hair." Lil stood and wandered down the hall. She shoved her feet into her boots and put on her coat before disappearing into the laundry room.

Shandra hurried down the hall to unlock and lock the back door once the woman left.

"I'm locking the door behind you. If you need to use the dryer again, you'll have to bring a key with you." Shandra opened the back door.

"I'll not bother you anymore tonight." Lil tipped her spiked white hair toward the door. "This have anything to do with Ryan staying away?"

The woman had an uncanny knack for figuring things out. "Yes. But I'm not at liberty to explain. Just be wary of any strangers coming here or hanging out in the woods on a snowmobile."

Lil stopped and kicked the door shut. "I thought I heard one of those things on the property today. About mid-afternoon."

A chill whisked up her spine. Had the person already found the connection between her and Ryan? "Did you see anything?"

"No. Just heard it when I was leading Sunshine

98

into the barn." Lil stared at her with one eye squinted. "Thought it was peculiar to hear one of them on this property but thought it could be an echo of someone cutting down wood over at the neighbors."

"How far off did it sound? Did it stop or keep going?" Maybe it was just the neighbors cutting firewood.

"Didn't sound like it stopped but thinking on it, I would swear it was moving."

Then it was a snowmobile on the property. "Up in our trees or down, like along the road?"

Lil's eyes narrowed and her face scrunched into her digging in and fighting expression. "It was up in the woods. That no-account was trespassing." She grabbed the door handle and pulled the door open. "Tomorrow, I'll go see where he came from and where he was going."

She grabbed the older woman's coat sleeve to stop her. "No. I'll call Ryan and let him know. You stay here and take care of Sunshine." She stared down in the older woman's eyes. "Promise me you won't go looking for the person."

Lil glared back at her with her jaw set stubbornly.

"Lil, if it's the man I think it is, he's killed two people already. Please, don't go looking for him." The strong-willed woman had become her eccentric aunt since they both started living on the mountain together. It would be like losing family if anything happened to her.

"I'll stay put, but only because Sunshine needs me. Not because I'm scared of no trespasser."

"I know you aren't scared of him. But I am, and I would feel better if you stayed close to the buildings."

She would also feel safer with the woman nearby. She was a crack shot, and as she'd stated, not afraid of anything.

Lil stepped out into the cold night air. Shandra closed the door and locked it, watching the woman until she disappeared between the studio and the barn.

Ryan needed to know about the snowmobile. She glanced at the clock on the microwave. One. She turned off the lights as she walked through the house and straight to the table in her bedroom where her phone sat.

Rather than wake him, she text. *Lil heard a snowmobile in our woods this afternoon.*

She walked into the bathroom to prepare for bed. Returning to the bedroom, *Dream a Little Dream*, jingled from her phone. She knew who it was without looking.

"You should be sleeping," she answered.

"When did Lil hear the snowmobile?" He skipped right over her scolding.

"She said mid-afternoon. No specific time. And it was definitely on the property." She half-laughed. "She wanted to go out looking for the person tomorrow, but I told her to stay close to the buildings."

"That's wise. I'd prefer you came into town where there are more people to keep an eye on you," he said.

"That didn't help the marshal. The town was overflowing with people on Saturday and looked what happened to him."

When Ryan didn't respond, she added. "I'll be fine. I'm more worried about you. Get some sleep so you can outsmart this guy. Good night."

"Night. Be careful," he responded.

"Go to sleep." She slid the phone to off and slipped under the covers. Maybe Ella would come to her and help her keep Ryan safe.

Sheba wandered into the room and hopped onto the bed, taking up the side where Ryan slept.

Shandra laughed. "You're enjoying Ryan being away, aren't you, you big goofball." She ruffled the dog's ears and turned out the light.

~*~

Ella did appear in her dream. *But rather than feeling comforted by her grandmother's appearance, her nerves felt like they lived on the top of her skin. Everyone who touched her sent a jolt of wariness coursing through her. She spied Ryan in the distance. Trying to make her way to him, her feet dragged through the knee-high snow, making her so tired she couldn't reach him. She fell into the snow. Air whooshed out of her lungs and she gasped for air. She pushed with her arms and shoved her body up.*

"Woof!" a wet wide tongue slid across her cheek.

Shandra pushed out of the dream. Sheba had her paws on her chest, making it hard to breathe.

"What is it girl?" She glanced at the clock. Six. "Ugh. It's too early. We went to bed late. Go back to sleep." She shoved the large furry beast off of her and tried to relax and go back to sleep.

"Woof!" This time she didn't lick or put her feet on Shandra. Her nose was pointed toward the window.

The windows in her bedroom faced the forest behind the house. She sat up and twisted around to peer out into the darkness. Only there wasn't darkness. Several lights bobbed through the trees.

Chapter Thirteen

Ryan led the search happening in the forest behind Shandra's house. He couldn't sleep after Shandra's call the night before until he'd contacted the Search and Rescue commander. He'd scheduled to meet several of the members at Shandra's at six in the morning. They had to discover where the snowmobile tracks went to before the next snow storm came through that afternoon.

"Ryan! Ryan!" Shandra's voice rang clear in the cold December morning.

He spun around and caught Shandra in his flashlight beam. She was bundled up like a small child heading out for a day of sledding.

"What are you doing out here?" he asked, trudging through the deep snow back to her.

"Sheba woke me. She must have heard you all pull

up out front. Then I looked out the window and saw the lights. I didn't know what to think until I spotted your work SUV."

Leeland hadn't been very happy with the 4 a.m. call requesting he pick Ryan up at five from the Huckleberry Police Station.

"You shouldn't be out here," he said, watching the others moving farther into the forest.

"Did you get more leads? Is that why you're out here so early?"

She stood close enough he caught a whiff of her herbal shampoo. It took all his strength to not wrap her in his arms and indulge in a moment of saneness.

"No leads. There's a storm coming in this afternoon. I wanted to get a bearing on where the snowmobile tracks came from and were headed. Since we found his camp, he may be looking for a place to set up another one." He waved toward the house. "Go back inside and pretend we aren't out here."

Her golden eyes glowed in the light of his flashlight. "Only if you promise to come in when you come back and update me."

With each moment of silence that hung between them as he fashioned his reply, her smile faded.

"Please. It can't hurt for you to come in for half an hour and visit with me."

She'd never pleaded for anything since he'd met her. That she was so close to begging, showed him how much thirty minutes with him would mean to her.

"Okay, but I won't be alone. Captain Leeland is my appointed guardian." He tried to make light of the fact he had to have the captain along with him.

"That's fine. I just want to have some time with

you and know you are safe." She stood on her toes and kissed his cheek. "Go find out where this guy is so we can get back to our lives."

Before he did something stupid, like grab her and kiss her like he'd wanted to do since she found the marshal's body, he pivoted and trudged into the trees following the bobbing lights of the others.

After walking twenty feet, he looked back to make sure Shandra had returned to the house. She stood inside the patio doors, still dressed in her snow clothes, watching him. He waved and hurried through the deepening snow to find the others.

A hundred yards up the mountain side from the buildings, the six volunteers and Leeland stood with their lights all beamed on a spot on the ground.

"What did you find?" he asked, approaching the group.

"From the fur and blood, I'd say something killed and ate a rabbit here," Maxwell Treat said. He was the son and partner of the local mortician and part of the search and rescue volunteers. Ryan hadn't been surprised when the big man showed up that morning to help. But he had been pleasantly surprised at how protective he was of Shandra. It seemed he deemed her his Ruthie's best friend and nothing was going to happen to her on his watch.

"Has anyone ran into snowmobile tracks?" he asked, glancing around at all the faces.

"Not yet." Leeland glanced back down the mountain. "She say how far away it sounded?"

"Lil's the one who heard it yesterday. I haven't questioned her." Ryan knew he should have done that as soon as they arrived. But he'd herded everyone into the woods hoping to avoid waking Shandra. He knew she'd been up just as late as he had the night before.

"With the snow and clear day she could have heard something like that a mile away," said Bernie Soffit, a local business owner.

Ryan waved his flashlight beam up the side of the mountain. "Spread out and keep going. When we've gone a mile, we'll come back down."

Everyone nodded and spread out heading up the side of the mountain. He knew the mountain better than anyone else out here, having ridden and walked it with Shandra. There was a gate on the east side that came in from the neighbors in that direction. Above her property was all National Forest. To the west was another neighbor. But there weren't any gates there. He had enough experience in law enforcement to know the suspect they were looking for wouldn't let a fence get in his way.

They traveled another twenty minutes when someone called out to his left.

As the world started lightening to grays and shadowed blacks, he and the other bobbing flashlights converged on a spot where Keith Upton stood.

"These look like snowmobile tracks to me," he said, pointing his light to the ground.

Ryan pulled out his phone and flipped through the photos of the scene where William Perry had been killed. He'd taken photos of the tracks there and the ones at the camp he and Leeland had discovered the day before.

He held the phone down just above the tracks. Everyone leaned in and looked.

"Those look identical to me." Leeland's voice

wasn't triumphant. He knew as well as Ryan what finding them here meant. Shandra was in danger.

"They're headed east," said Treat.

Ryan nodded. "I'll follow them. The rest of you go on home. Thank you for all your help." He took one step and a hand fell on both his shoulders. Treat had one and Leeland had the other.

"You're not following those by yourself." Leeland stepped in front of him, blocking his way. "We'll do this properly." He pulled out his phone and frowned.

"There's limited reception once you get fifty yards beyond Shandra's place," Ryan said.

Leeland pointed to three of the volunteers. "You three go back down and call Sheriff Oldham at the Weippe Sheriff's Department. Tell him we found the tracks and that we need more deputies up here. Also that Greer, myself, and the rest of the search team are following the tracks."

They nodded and headed back down the mountain.

Treat stood beside the tracks. "Looks like we're tracking this thing." He took off, his long legged stride a half a length longer than anyone else in the group.

"Don't let him get too far ahead," Ryan said, scrambling to fall in behind Treat. He didn't want the big-hearted man to get killed on his behalf.

~*~

Shandra was at the island in her kitchen sipping tea when Lil banged through the back door.

"What's with all the vehicles in the yard?" she asked, walking over and pouring herself a cup of coffee.

"They're out searching for the snowmobile tracks." Shandra glanced at the clock on the microwave. She'd

106

talked to Ryan an hour ago. How far up did they have to go to find the tracks? Or had the whole thing been a mistake?

"Good. I don't like the idea of trespassers on the mountain." Lil chugged the hot liquid. "Since there's people here, I'll head into town for that heating blanket. I'll get to the store as it opens and hightail it back. That way you aren't left alone here."

"How did Sunshine do last night?" She wanted to think of anything other than Ryan being on the mountain with the possibility of running into the man out to kill him.

"She made it through and seems to be moving a bit easier this morning. I think keeping her warm through the night is the key." Lil set the mug in the sink and headed for the back door. "Be back in two hours."

"Drive careful. You don't have to risk your life by driving too fast on the packed snow."

Lil grinned and closed the door.

Shandra sighed. Sometimes watching over Lil felt like she had a teenaged daughter rather than a sixty-plus employee.

She decided to make soup and rolls to keep her busy. It would also feed the searchers when they returned. Giving her the perfect way to ask questions.

Car doors slamming caught her attention. She looked out the kitchen window and spotted someone talking on a radio while two other people sat in a vehicle.

She snatched her coat off the hook by the back door and hurried out.

The man on the radio spotted her first. He waved. A glance at the vehicle and she recognize a couple of the men from Huckleberry. The man on the radio put it in the vehicle and walked around to her.

"Miss Higheagle, I'm Bernie Soffit. I own the deli in town."

"Mr. Soffit, please call me Shandra. You have delicious food. I've shopped there when entertaining." She held out her hand. "Did you find the snowmobile tracks?"

"Yes. Captain Leeland sent us down to call the sheriff for more deputies and to let him know what was happening." He rubbed his hands together.

"I'm sorry, you must all be freezing. Come in. I have soup on and rolls about to go in the oven. Plus plenty of hot coffee." She waved to the house.

He looked like he was about to refuse.

"Come on. It's the least I can do after Detective Greer called you out here at the crack of dawn." She tapped on the window of the vehicle.

The man next to the window rolled it down.

"I have soup, coffee, and fresh rolls. Come in and warm up." She started toward the back door. The sound of a car door closing and the squeak of footsteps on the packed snow behind her made her smile.

She'd pump them for every bit of information they had about what was happening up on the mountain.

Chapter Fourteen

Ryan stood at the fence line between Shandra's property and the neighbors on the east. As he'd figured, whoever rode the snowmobile had pulled two fence posts over, laying the fence down in the snow and driving over it. What he didn't like was the fact a hundred yards after they'd started following the tracks, it was apparent the person had ridden down the mountain side and back up. As if he were looking for the best way to get to the house.

"Do you know who lives over here?" Leeland asked after they'd crossed the fence.

"Not anymore. The husband was killed over a year ago, and I heard the wife sold the place." The memory of Shandra finding that body, sent his feet moving faster. He pushed by Treat and strode alongside the tracks.

"Wait, we can't barge onto someone's property," Leeland said loud enough for him to hear but not carry.

He stopped and faced Leeland and the other three. "We're out to apprehend a suspect in two murders. I don't think anyone would care when we could be saving their life."

"I think it would be best to regroup and visit with the neighbors and ask if we could look around." Leeland, nodded back to the fence. "Come on. We'll use Miss Higheagle's house as the base. She'll be safe and we'll have a place to work from."

Ryan didn't like aborting the tracking. For all they knew the guy could have driven back into Shandra's property from a spot lower on the mountain.

"He could be somewhere in the forest right now watching everything we do." He had to voice his opinion.

"He could. But he won't have Shandra as a target with all of us there. We'll catch him. It will just take time." Leeland motioned for everyone to start walking back.

"At least, we can follow the fence and see if he crossed over at a lower spot." Ryan headed down hill at the fence line.

"We gotta go down anyway," Treat said, behind him.

Ryan didn't wait to see if anyone else followed him. When he stopped to take a breather, everyone was with him. Leeland bringing up the back.

"Not much farther and there's a gate between the two places." Ryan drank from his water bottle and started downward again.

His heart stalled at the sight of several snowmobile

tracks crossing through the open gate. He stopped and stared at the tracks. There was no telling how many times the machine had passed through the gate or which way it had last traveled.

Leeland pulled out his phone and took photos. "Come on. Let's get to the house and get a plan in action." He started down the fence line.

"No. Follow the tracks. The house is this way. Following the fence will take you down to the county road." Ryan felt the handle of his Glock on his belt and walked in the snowmobile tracks. He didn't care if the son-of-a-bitch knew they were on to him. His main focus was keeping Shandra safe.

~*~

Shandra was disappointed in how little the three men knew about their trip out here. They were told to look for snowmobile tracks. They weren't sure why, but they did what they were asked to do. Locate the tracks.

She filled the coffee pot, making more coffee. Sheba sniffed the men and received a pat on the head from each. She sat next to the youngest man who had tossed her a bite of his roll.

"The soup was delicious," Bernie said. "We need to find out if we can get back to our jobs." He stood, grabbing the coat he'd hung over the back of the stool before he'd sat down.

"I understand. Is there any way to contact the rest of them to see when they'll be here?" She was getting anxious about Ryan following the tracks and running into the killer.

"If they're in radio range I can try them." He motioned to the other two. "Come on. We should get going."

Shandra pulled on her coat and followed them to the pickup.

Bernie pulled a radio out of the vehicle and talked into it. Voices crackled. He asked for their location. More crackling voices. "We're headed out of here. Haven't seen any deputies yet." Voices crackled over the radio. He glanced up at her. "Yes, sir." He put the radio in the vehicle and said something to the other two. They stepped out of the vehicle.

"We'll be hanging out here until the others show up. The detective thinks it will be about an hour." Bernie motioned for her to return to the house.

There was a reason Ryan asked these men to stay with her. Were they chasing the guy to the house? Back inside, she refilled their coffee mugs and started mixing up cookies.

Once they were all seated at the island, she asked, "Why did Ryan ask you to stay here?"

Bernie didn't look at her. He ran his thumb up and down the handle on his cup. "He didn't really say. Just that he didn't want you left alone."

Her heart stammered in her chest. He thought the man was out there somewhere watching, waiting for her to be left alone.

"I see." She kept her tone even and dived into making cookies.

The men talked among themselves about sports and hunting. She tuned them out as she mixed the dough.

The back door banged opened, making her jump.

"What are all of you doing in here?" Lil asked, in an accusing tone.

The three men stared at her employee. They had good reason. She held a shotgun on them.

"They are part of the search and rescue," Shandra said when she found her voice.

"What they doin' in here instead of out on the mountain?" Lil hadn't lowered the rifle.

"They were sent down to call in more deputies and stay with me." Shandra walked over to her employee and tipped the barrel down to the floor. "Put your rifle in the laundry room and join us for some fresh cookies."

The ornery woman cradled the rifle in her arms. "I'm not staying for cookies. I have chores to do."

"Be careful," Shandra whispered, before the woman swung around and walked out the door.

The men all relaxed and quietly talked among themselves. She was getting antsy waiting for the rest of the group to come back.

She slid a pan of cookies into the oven and turned to put dough on another tray.

Sheba's loud barking, signaled someone approached the house. She hadn't barked earlier because she knew Lil's old truck, but someone else was driving up. The bark was her heralding company call.

"Will one of you pull these out of the oven when the timer goes off?" she asked.

Bernie nodded.

She walked to the great room and peered out the window. Two deputy sheriff cars were parked next to Ryan's SUV. She opened the door as two deputies and Sheriff Oldham approached. Pretty soon they would have all of the Weippe County Sheriff's Office on her property.

"Good morning, Miss Higheagle. We'd like permission to set up in your home until we capture the person suspected of killing two people." The sheriff removed his hat as he spoke.

"I guess that's okay. I've never had my home taken over by authorities before." She stepped back and the two deputies behind the sheriff walked in carrying boxes.

Sheriff Oldham ushered her inside as the deputies exited. "That coffee smells good."

"Come into the kitchen. I have cookies baking." She hurried back to the kitchen and found a pan on the cooling rack and one in the oven. She smiled at Bernie. "Thank you."

He nodded.

"Men, now that my deputies and I are here, you may go." Sheriff Oldham shook each man's hand and thanked them for their help this morning while Shandra filled a mug with coffee and a plate with cookies.

The men gathered their coats and left by the back door. The room felt empty and quiet as the sheriff returned to the great room and directed the deputies with the second batch of boxes they'd brought in.

Shandra stared out the kitchen window, wondering about Ryan and the others.

~*~

The sheriff radioed Leeland just as Ryan had crossed a path in the snow made by a human and not an animal. From his best judgement, they were only a couple hundred feet from the barnyard area. The brush and trees were thick in this area. Thick enough to cover anyone hanging around here watching.

"I don't like seeing this trail," he said to Leeland.

The man nodded. "Everyone stay alert."

Ryan pulled his Glock from the holster on his belt

and followed the foot path. He was pretty sure this path had been used more than once. He hoped they found the person. Though it was hard to know how many people could be out to get him. Members from three gangs had died that night. They had all sworn revenge. But he had a feeling only one would actually seek blood for blood. One of the young men who died and, had been the first to take him in when he infiltrated the gang, was the brother of the Gangsters Disciples leader.

The path he followed stopped behind a clump of five-foot tall bushes. At the base of the bushes, someone had dug out the snow and made a cozy den. Several horse blankets lined the ground.

Ryan's first reaction was to jerk out the blankets, but this was how they would catch him. That was if he didn't see their tracks.

"He's been here. Made a nice den for himself." He stepped back and pointed to the base of the bushes. "We need to get out of here without leaving more tracks." It would mean back tracking all the way back to where they started following this path.

"I take it that building is one of Miss Higheagle's?" Leeland waved to the back of the studio.

"Yes. That's her studio." He pointed to the left. "Those are her corrals, horses, and barn." The only good thing about where the person had picked to watch her, he couldn't see the house or into the windows.

"I'll radio and let Oldham know we'll be a bit longer getting to the house. It wouldn't do to put surveillance on this spot until we can pinpoint it for the others."

He agreed. Leeland radioed the new information as they started back up the path.

His legs burned from the fatigue of walking up and down the mountain in the two feet of snow. But knowing they would soon have this threat taken away, kept him moving. Back at the snowmobile trail, he followed it east back to the fence before heading downhill along the fence line. After a hundred yards he stopped, allowing everyone else to catch up to him. He'd been cutting the path for the others to follow. His legs were feeling like wet noodles, but they had a good half-a-mile to go to reach the buildings.

"You want me to take the lead?" Treat asked.

"You don't know which way to go," he replied, stuffing his empty water bottle into his pack.

"I was one of the people who came when Mr. Randal was killed. I know this part of the property pretty well." Treat stepped around him and headed through the trees.

Having the big man break a trail gave his legs a rest. Another half hour and the barn came into view. Treat walked to the back corner.

Everyone sped up the pace walking to the front, stomping the snow from their boots when they hit the bladed ground in front of the barn.

The barn door flew open and Lil stood in the opening, a shotgun aimed at them.

"Lil, put that thing away before you shoot someone," he said, dismissing the woman and heading for the back door of the house.

Sheba barked and hid behind the corner of the studio.

"Hey girl. It's me," Ryan said, noting the county vehicles filling Shandra's yard.

The big mutt loped over to him and would have

knocked him down if he hadn't been ready for her wide chest bumping into him.

Shandra appeared at the back door. Her smile was welcoming even if her gaze held worry.

Leeland was telling the search and rescue members to go home.

"Don't leave!" Shandra called.

Chapter Fifteen

Shandra couldn't hide her relief at the sight of Ryan with Sheba. But she also didn't miss the fatigue on all the men's faces. "Come in, all of you. I have soup, rolls, and cookies."

Ryan was the first to the door. He kissed her on the cheek. "That sounds good. We're all pretty tired." He walked on through and into the laundry room, where he began taking off his outerwear.

She greeted Captain Leeland, Maxwell, who gave her a hug, and the other two men with them. "Put your snowy things in the laundry room and come into the kitchen."

Ryan put an arm around her shoulders and walked into the kitchen with her.

"Did you find him?" she asked in a whisper, knowing he wasn't supposed to talk about his cases with her.

"We found where he's hiding." He picked up a roll. "I need to go let the sheriff know so he can send someone out to watch." He bit the roll and strolled into the great room as if her house was the sheriff's department every day.

Captain Leeland helped himself to a cup of coffee before wandering into the other room. Maxwell and the other two took seats at the island. She ladled soup into their bowls, shoved the plate of rolls and butter their direction, and started filling mugs with coffee. The whole time her mind was wondering what was being talked about in the other room.

Ryan returned to the kitchen and took a seat next to Maxwell. She served him soup and waited for him to say something.

"We hiked all over that mountain," Maxwell said.

"Did you see any wildlife?" she asked, easing into what she really wanted to know.

"Some birds, the tail end of some deer," one of the other men said.

"Didn't find the wild animal we were lookin' for," added Maxwell.

She turned her gaze on Ryan. "Do you think you'll get him?"

He captured her hand in his. "Yes. If he doesn't realize we're on to him, we'll get him."

"I heard someone leave." She couldn't come right out and ask the questions she wanted to ask. Not with the other men in the room.

"That was Ron. He's going to get up in the barn loft and watch for the suspect to return. He'll radio when that happens."

"The loft? He's right behind the barn?" Her first thoughts went to Lil staying in the barn alone at night. "I'll have to make Lil stay in here with me until you catch him." She spun to get her coat and warn her friend.

Ryan caught her arm. "You aren't going out there. I'm sure Ron had to explain why he was climbing up in the loft of the barn. She'll be safe with our surveillance."

What he said was true, but she didn't like feeling so helpless with a house full of lawmen.

Someone cleared their throat, reminding her she stood in the kitchen staring into Ryan's eyes.

"Thank you for the food, Shandra. We're heading out of here." Maxwell slapped Ryan on the shoulder. "Good luck catching this guy."

"Thanks." Ryan didn't let loose of her arm or drop his gaze from hers.

They remained that way while the men put on their boots and coats and left, closing the back door quietly behind them.

Ryan pulled her into his arms, holding her close.

She didn't want to show her vulnerability, but she clung to him as if her feet were sliding off a precipice.

"Don't worry. We'll get this guy," he whispered and kissed her temple.

"But is he the only one?" She pushed against his chest and peered into his eyes. "Will we be reliving this in six months, a year?"

"I hope not. If that's what it looks like will happen, I'll move and stay away from you and my family."

The finality of his words struck like a fist to her belly. The air whooshed out of her and her mind spun.

He would leave to keep them safe. His sacrifice was immeasurable. And something she didn't want him to do.

"No, you aren't leaving. Ever. We'll get through this together. I'll ask Ella for guidance."

He shook his head. "She can't keep me safe."

"But she can show us the danger."

The voices of the men in the other room reminder her they weren't alone. She moved back into his arms and whispered, "I had a dream last night. Ella was there. So were you. But I couldn't get to you." She wasn't going to tell him she couldn't get to him because she was smothering. That would only make him more worried about her.

"Don't you see? That's her saying I need to go away. Someplace you and my family can't be associated with me." His voice rasped with emotion.

"No. If you go away, they will only come after your family to get you out of hiding. They have to know everything about you by now."

"Excuse me," Sheriff Oldham said, from the doorway.

Ryan released her slowly and turned to his boss. "Yes?"

"They found fingerprints that match a gang member on some of the items you retrieved from the camp area." The sheriff turned and walked away.

"I need to go see what they've come up with." He stood. "I'm not going anywhere yet."

She stared at his back. Or ever. She'd bring Grandmother into her dreams tonight and ask for her help.

~*~

Ryan stared at the computer screen sitting on Shandra's dining room table. The photo didn't remind him of anyone he'd known while in the gang, but the description fit the person Shandra had encountered in Huckleberry. His name was PeeWee Woodbridge. He'd been pulled in by Chicago P.D. on numerous counts of indecent exposure and two assaults with a knife. It appeared the Disciples had hired him to take care of Shawn O'Grady.

"We have him flying in from Chicago to Spokane. From there I'm not sure how he got to Weippe County. His flight left several hours before Deputy U.S. Marshal Winston got on a plane in Chicago." Oldham glanced up. "Like they knew what was happening before it happened."

Ryan wasn't surprised. The fact the gangs seemed to know every move the police made was why he'd been sent in undercover with only one person knowing his true identity.

The jazz tune on Shandra's phone jingled. The sound came from her bedroom.

"Your phone's ringing," he called toward the kitchen.

She ran by them, her moccasin slippers barely making a sound on the wood flooring.

"Hi Ted. Oh, I've been busy in the kitchen and my phone was in the bedroom."

He knew listening in to other people's conversations was wrong, but when it came to Shandra, her safety was all that mattered. Knowing it was Ted, her best friend's husband and one of the gallery owners who purchased her art, he went back to skimming the information on PeeWee.

"No. Today isn't a good day to bring him out." Shandra appeared at the door of her bedroom still talking on the phone. "Why?" She glanced at him for help.

"Tell him because you have to go to town," he said, wandering over and listening to the conversation by leaning his head next to hers.

"I have to go to town."

"You were just in here yesterday. Surely you could stay home so I can bring Mr. Sterling out. He is looking at three of your pieces in the gallery but wants to see the process." Ted's tone was a bit demanding for Ryan's liking.

He took the phone from Shandra. "Ted, this is Ryan."

The man sucked in air before saying, "I don't see why Shandra can't allow this potential client to come see her studio today. He's only here on vacation and will be going home soon."

"She isn't available today. Check back with her tomorrow." He pushed the off button and handed the phone to Shandra. "Everyone has to stay away from here until we get this guy." He tucked a strand of her hair behind her ear. "I wish you were in town instead of here."

She slipped the phone into her back pocket. "I'm not going anywhere. Captain Leeland, you haven't eaten. Come into the kitchen and I'll get you a bowl of soup."

Leeland followed Shandra into the kitchen.

Sheriff Oldham turned to Ryan. "What was that call all about?"

"Some guy vacationing here wanted to see her

studio. That was one of the gallery owners, a friend of Shandra's, trying to get him out here today." Ryan had wondered about Ted back when Naomi had been a suspect in another gallery owner's murder. He'd been a bit pushy then, too. He was surprised Shandra hadn't noticed. After her experience in college, he would have thought she'd stay away from that type, or at least push back.

"What do you know about this guy?" Oldham settled back down in front of the computer.

"Ted? He's a bit pushy for my liking—"

"No," Oldham cut in. "The guy wanting to see the studio."

"Nothing. Ted called him Mr. Sterling. Shandra had dinner with the client, Ted, and Naomi, Ted's wife." He wondered if Oldham was being overly suspicious. Or if he should be more suspicious.

"Don't you find it a bit of a coincidence that this guy is hot after her art at this time?" The sheriff pulled out his phone. "I'll call the lodge and see what they have on him."

Ryan nodded and wandered into the kitchen. Guess he better start asking Shandra some questions.

Chapter Sixteen

Shandra liked Captain Leeland. He had a kind face and was eager to talk about his family.

"Does your wife ever worry about you? You know when you're doing things like this?" She'd never had a chance to talk to the wife of a law man. She wondered if the fear ever went away.

"All the time. But we've discussed the fact this is what I want to do. It helps people. She's a teacher so she understands wanting to help." He waved half a roll at her. "You and my Julie should get together. I'll have her call and set up a time you two can meet." He nodded to the other room as Ryan walk through the door. "If you're going to hang around with Ryan you could use a friend who knows what it's like to be married to a man in law enforcement."

"What's this about marriage?" Ryan asked, his

gaze locked on her.

"I was telling Shandra if she plans to hang around with you she might want a woman's view of being married to someone in our profession." The captain wiped his mouth, stood, and picked up his dishes, carrying them to the sink. "That was delicious. Thanks." He walked into the other room leaving them alone.

Her heart thudded in her chest as he continued to stare at her. What was going on behind those brown eyes?

He finally spoke. "What can you tell me about Mr. Sterling?"

It took her several seconds to comprehend what he'd asked. She thought he was going to say something about their future, not bring up a man she'd met once. "He…uh…not much. Why?"

"It seems curious that he is so adamant to get out here and see your process. How many in the years you've been selling have insisted on seeing where you work?" He leaned against the counter, his arms crossed.

"Two or three people a year like to come see the studio and ask questions about making my own clay. He said he's been ripped off by art investments before and wanted to make sure I was the real deal." She didn't see anything wrong with that. She'd known some shady art dealers over the years.

"What does he do? Where is he from? How did he pick Huckleberry Lodge?" He pushed away from the counter and walked toward her. "Right now we have to question any stranger's motives."

She shook her head. "How can you live worrying that everyone you don't know is going to harm you?"

He reached out and drew her up against him. "I hadn't until that FBI agent recognized me. I'll figure out how to keep from looking over my shoulder. I might have to go to Chicago and talk with the gang leaders, we'll see. Right now, my focus is making sure no one harms you or my family." He held her away from him. "What do you know about this Sterling guy?"

"Not much. Ted and Naomi know more. We talked art the other night. I think he is from Seattle. He said he was in import and export. He evaded most business question, like some of the men my stepfather had shady dealings with." She moved to the sink to put the dirty dishes in the dishwasher. "Do you think he's from a gang? He was dressed in fancy clothes and talked like someone who had a quality education."

"We're doing a background check on him." Ryan walked over and picked up the dishes she rinsed, placing them in the dishwasher. "I think it would be a good idea for you to visit with Julie Leeland. She's been a cop's wife for a long time."

She glanced over at him. The solemn set of his face didn't tell her if he wanted her to know what she was getting into or hoping she'd run.

~*~

The afternoon dragged, waiting to see if PeeWee returned to his den under the bushes. When Ryan couldn't stand being cooped up any longer, he wandered out to the barn. He wanted to see if Ron had picked a good vantage point or if they'd been sitting in here waiting for someone who had already snuggled in.

Lil met him as he opened the barn door. "What are you doing out here?"

"I came to give Ron a break." He continued toward the ladder leading up to the loft.

"You're the reason that deputy is up there. And you're the reason Shandra is in danger." She stood in front of the ladder, keeping him from going up without forcefully moving her.

"Yeah. I am." He stared at the older woman. Her green eyes narrowed. "But even if I left that wouldn't make her any less of a target. The people who want me dead already know I care for her. They'd just use her as bait to get me to come back."

She nodded. "But she has me to see that no one gets to her."

He put a hand on the woman's shoulder. "For all our differences, I can honestly say, I am thankful every day that you are here to protect her."

The woman's eyes widened and her chin quivered a moment. But as fleeting as he saw the softening the woman hardened her stare and her chin. She stepped away from the loft. "I was told to stay away from the back of the barn. How am I to take care of the horses?"

"If all goes as planned, you should be back to normal by this evening." He grabbed a rung of the ladder and planted a foot. At the top, he spotted Deputy Trap sitting on an upturned wooden box, the wooden window cover was open slightly and a spotting scope stuck through the crack.

"See anything?" he asked.

"A couple of deer, rabbits, turkeys. This place is a hunter's paradise." He nodded to the scope. "I can barely make out the path leading behind the bushes. Haven't seen your boy. But I thought I heard a snowmobile back there about thirty minutes ago."

128

Ryan thought about their hike. "If he didn't figure out someone has been on the trail he should be showing soon. If that was him on a snowmobile."

The sound of a vehicle arriving out front drew Ryan's attention. He was torn between staying here with the possibility of apprehending the gang member or seeing who had driven up.

Sheba's barking pulled him to find out who had arrived.

"Need a break," he asked.

"I'm good." Ron had one eye to the scope.

"Let us know if he returns or you need a break." He raised his thumb.

Ryan headed down the ladder and out of the barn. It was a state police SUV. That would mean Whorter had finished interviewing the neighbors. He hurried to the back door and slipped out of his outerwear.

Several voices were talking in the great room. He strode down the hall and encountered Whorter, Oldham, Leeland, and a man he knew and wanted to strangle. They all turned at his entrance.

"What the hell are you doing here?" he demanded of FBI Agent Frank Weatherly.

The man put his hands up and had the decency to look embarrassed. "I can understand why you're upset."

"Upset? You haven't seen me upset. You put everyone I love in jeopardy because you couldn't let it go when you thought you knew me." Ryan turned to his superiors. "This is the jackass who dug into who I was and let my whereabouts get leaked to the gangs. I don't want him here."

Oldham started to say something when Shandra walked into the room carrying a tray with a pot of coffee and cups for everyone. She set them on the dining room table and moved to Ryan's side.

He stared into her golden eyes. "How could you let him in this house knowing he's the person who turned our lives upside down?"

"He couldn't have known what would happen by checking out how he remembered you." She rubbed a hand up and down his arm. "If he hadn't have recognized you, you would still be worrying and wondering. Maybe we can get this taken care of once and for all."

He knew she was grasping at a life without fear, but being married to a man in his profession, she wouldn't find that peace until he retired.

"I still don't like it." He glared at the FBI agent.

Oldham cleared his throat. "You may not like it but he's here to investigate the murder of the deputy marshal. Right now we think we have the man's next move figured out," the sheriff said to Weatherly.

Shandra caught Ryan's attention. She tipped her head towards the forest.

He shook his head slightly in response to her unasked question, 'was the man out there?'

"May I go out to my studio? I've done all I can in here, but I have lots of work I could be doing out there." She asked him, but glanced around to all the men.

He opened his mouth to answer but Sheriff Oldham beat him.

"It would be best if you stayed in the house until we have the suspect apprehended." His fatherly appearance and softly spoken words had her nodding her head.

"I'll be in the kitchen." She glanced at him before heading down the hall.

He understood she wanted to keep her hands busy and not think about what was going on. He pulled his gaze from her and found the others watching him.

"It's hard on her. She's used to being out in the studio working, not catering to law enforcement."

"What did you find out?" he asked Whorter.

"The neighbors toward town have noticed a buzzing sound they would equate to a snowmobile the last few days. There is no one living on the east side. The place is boarded up and a "For Sale" sign is at the county road."

"Did you check the out buildings?" He had a feeling the suspect had holed up at the abandoned place.

"I sent two patrolmen to keep an eye on things." Whorter motioned to the other man.

The radio on the table crackled. Oldham picked it up. "Oldham."

"Our man just hunkered down under the bushes."

Everyone in the room, headed for their coats.

Chapter Seventeen

Shandra watched as the lawmen hurried into their coats and boots, then huddled together in her front yard before scattering through the trees on either side of the buildings.

She hugged Sheba and sat in her favorite chair by the glass patio doors, waiting and watching the forest. The afternoon was waning. Sunlight only touched the top of the trees, down underneath the big pine boughs dusk had gathered, making it even harder for her to see anyone.

Her heart raced as she listened for gunshots.

Sheba squirmed from her grasp and laid down in front of the unlit fireplace. Whether it gave off warmth or not, the big dog preferred stretching out on the slate in front of the stove.

A glance at the clock said they'd been gone an

hour. From what she understood of the bits of conversation she'd heard, they didn't have to go very far.

A jingling jazz tune made her jump. She pulled her cellphone from a back pocket and spotted a number she didn't recognize.

"Hello?"

"Miss Higheagle, this is Mick Sterling. I hope I'm not catching you at a bad time."

Ryan's suspicions swam in her head. "No, I'm not busy at the moment."

"Good. Is there any way I can persuade you to allow me to visit you tonight?"

"Th—" Before she could say any more he cut her off.

"I know it's short notice, but I'm being called back to Seattle, and I'd really like to take these pieces back with me when I go tomorrow. But…"

He left the rest unsaid. He'd told them all why he wanted to see her studio last night.

"Then you'll just have to make another trip to Huckleberry to see my studio. I give tours during the Winter Art Festival and during the Summer Brew Fest." She knew it could lose her sales by putting him off, but she'd rather lose a sale than Ryan.

"I see." His tone told her she had angered him. "I don't understand why you can't give me half an hour of your time in order to sell your pieces."

"And I don't understand why, if you like them so much you can't believe Ted, Naomi, and myself, when we say they are one of a kind, created by me, and from the clay on my property." She paused. "I would think if you are such a great businessman you would know

133

when people are being genuine with you and when they are fake."

He started to sputter.

"I'm sure with your knowledge of art for your business you would be interested in seeing other local artists at the festivals."

The sound of car doors and engines starting up drew her to the front window. The vehicles were all leaving, except Ryan's SUV. He stood beside the vehicle looking frustrated.

"I have to go." She dropped the conversation, slipped her feet into furry boots, and grabbed a coat before opening the door and hurrying over to Ryan.

"Did you get him?" she asked, stopping in front of him to get his attention.

"Yes." He glanced down at her. "I was ordered to stay here. Oldham said I'd be too emotional. You're damn right I'd be! The little creep killed two people and was sitting there waiting to get me and would have killed you." He grabbed her arms and pulled her tight to his chest, holding on as if she might blow away.

"I'm here, you're alive, they have the guy. Come on. Let's have a nice dinner." She pushed out of his embrace and led him into the house.

After they'd shed their coats and boots, he sat at the counter sipping beer as she made spaghetti for their dinner.

Halfway through dinner, Ryan's phone rang. He glanced at the number. Sheriff Oldham. "I'll be right back." He left the kitchen, wandering into the great room.

"Sheriff, did he crack?" he asked.

"He cracked but it's not what we thought. PeeWee

was sent here to follow you, learn all he could, and report back to someone else. He swears he didn't kill anyone. He knows there is someone in the area ready to kill you but he only talks to someone in Chicago. A Devin Moore."

Ryan's hair stood up at the name. Devin had been one of the people he'd been close to while undercover. His younger brother had been one of the fatalities. Betrayal was one of the biggest reasons for murder.

"Can Weatherly find out where Moore is? Of all the gangs who would want retribution, he would be the one." His mind raced to remember all he could about the Moores.

"He's on the phone and computer doing his best. But if the suspect we have in custody didn't kill the two, who did?" Skepticism wavered in Sheriff Oldham's voice.

"If PeeWee didn't kill Perry how did he end up with the man's snowmobile?" Ryan paced the great room. He wanted to interrogate the suspect himself. He'd get answers.

"Whorter is still working on that with him. The little prick is acting stupid." Frustration rang in his voice.

"I could come help."

"You stay where you are until we have more information." The line went silent.

Ryan shoved his phone back in the holder and stared out the patio doors, watching new snow flutter down to the ground.

Shandra walked up beside him. "Good news?"

He continued staring at the fluttering snow. "No."

Dream a Little Dream jingled from her phone.

Shandra moved to the coffee table and picked up her phone, glancing at the name. Ted.

"Hello Ted." She had a feeling she knew why the gallery owner was calling.

"Did you really refuse to allow Mick Sterling to come out to your studio tonight?"

"Yes. You don't know what has been going on here all day and I don't feel like repeating myself, but tonight was out of the question. If he doesn't buy my pieces I don't care." And she didn't. There would be other buyers. This day had been like walking around in a dream from a movie.

"How do you know that? You turning him down could have cost you future sales as well." Ted wasn't letting it go.

Ryan walked up beside her, his left brow arched in question.

"I'm sorry Mr. Sterling felt he had to call you when I turned him down. The answer is still no."

Ryan held up his hand and whispered, "Tell him if Mr. Sterling can come out here at…" He glanced at the clock on the mantle, "Eight. You'll give him a tour."

Shandra didn't understand but sighed. "If he can be here by eight tonight, I'll give him a tour."

"Excellent! But what changed your mind?"

She couldn't answer Ted's question because she still didn't want to have the man out. "It wasn't me—"

Ryan pulled the phone away from her face and shook his head. She took the hint. No one was to know he was here.

"Ryan had to leave," she said, searching his eyes for what he had planned.

"I'll call Mick and let him know I'll pick him up."

The phone went silent.

She put her hands on her hips and stared at Ryan. "What is going on? Not that long ago you told me to stay away from Mick Sterling. Now you want me to invite him late at night to the studio."

"I'll put my vehicle in the barn. You and Lil can meet this Sterling at the studio. I'll be around watching. I might recognize him. And if I do, I'll arrest him." Ryan's face became animated for the first time all day. "If this person is who I think he is, he'll be pretty mad when he sees me."

"And you find that funny." Her tone didn't hold back the irritation she felt.

"Not funny. If this is who I think it is, it won't be funny at all. He could be the person who brought me into the gang. That he brought in the mole should have lost him footing in the gangs, but it seems to have made him stronger." His gaze peered over her shoulder. "He is going to be out for my skin."

"I better make coffee and put together a plate of cookies to take out to the studio." She pivoted and headed to the kitchen, hoping Sterling wasn't the man Ryan thought he was.

Chapter Eighteen

Shandra sat in her chair in the studio where she composed many of the designs for her vases and waited for the sound of a vehicle approaching. She checked her phone again. It was five minutes later than the last check. 7:50.

"You keep checking that phone and you'll wear down the battery," Lil said, from over by the kiln. She was putting more of the coasters she'd glazed several days ago into the big round firing drum.

She knew Ryan had talked to Lil while Shandra was in the kitchen making coffee and putting together a platter of cookies. What he said, she didn't know. His SUV had disappeared and so had Ryan. It was probably best she didn't know where he hid. That way she couldn't give him away.

Sheba rose to her haunches under the glazing table

and gave a half-hearted woof.

"They must be here." She headed to the door and stepped out. Sheba brushed past her and disappeared between the studio and barn.

Ted and Mick were getting out of Ted's Tahoe.

"Over here!" she called, catching their attention when they started toward the house.

Ted waved and the two crunched across the snow-packed yard.

"Come in. I have coffee and cookies." She ushered the two inside.

"Ted, you know Lil. Mr. Sterling, this is my employee, Lil." Shandra made the introductions and noted Lil sizing the man up.

"Lil, pleased to meet you," Mr. Sterling held out his hand.

Lil shook and went back to filling the kiln.

"What are those?" he asked, walking over and picking up a glazed coaster.

"I etch Huckleberry Mountain in coasters made from the mountain's clay, and the local businesses sell them. It's a steady income in between my vases."

"That's a solid business strategy. Most artists aren't that business savvy."

His compliment shouldn't have warmed her as much as it did. Only Ryan had noticed she was more than a flighty artist.

"Thank you. Over here…" She walked over to the wall that held clay in the various stages of cleansing. "Is where the clay is kept." She picked up the raw product. "We brought this bucket in from behind the studio several days ago. We'll start the cleansing process as soon as it is completely thawed. When it is, we'll wash it several times, then spread it out on these boards." She pulled the boards out from behind the table. "The mud is spread thin on here and allowed to dry. Then I mix water with it and wedge it until it is malleable. And that's when I start making vases or coasters."

Mick had watched her the whole time, his eyes missing nothing. "I'm impressed. I do believe you use clay from the mountain and you are the real deal artist." His smile was wide, warm, and infectious.

She grinned back at him.

"That mean tomorrow we'll be selling you those art pieces you were interested in?" Ted asked.

"Definitely. I would also like to see each new piece before you send or sell it to anyone. I can see you are going to make a name for yourself." Mick held out his hand. "Impressive."

She shook his hand and offered him coffee and cookies.

The men took her up on her offer and were soon sitting at the two chairs looking through the notebook she had with photographs of every project she'd made and sold.

She glanced over her shoulder at Lil. The woman gave her a thumbs up and a nod to the stairs leading up to the apartment over the studio. She caught a glimpse of Ryan before he closed the apartment door.

Since he hadn't come charging down the stairs to apprehend the man, he must not be a threat. That made her feel good. After Mick said she had a head for business and he loved her art, she didn't want him to be the man out to kill Ryan.

"I like this piece. Is there any chance you would

replicate this only color it with sunset colors?" Mick had his finger on one of her earlier pieces.

The exact same piece Ryan had bought at the Summer Art Fest two years ago. Mick stared at her waiting for her reply.

"I could do that. After I finish what I'm working on now." She glanced over to the pottery wheel draped with a large white drop cloth.

"Any chance we'd get a peek at your work in progress?" he asked.

"No. No one gets to see that other than Lil because she's in and out of here all day long."

"What about Ryan? Do you let him see your work in progress?" Ted asked.

Shandra wondered if she imagined a subtle change in Mick.

"Who is Ryan?" Mick asked.

"A man who means a lot to me. And no, even Ryan doesn't get to see my pieces until I'm finished and happy with the way it looks." She glared at Ted. He rarely cared what was happening in her life outside of her art.

"I see. This Ryan. Does he know how lucky he is to have you?" Mick put a hand on his chest. "Because if he doesn't, I'll gladly take his place."

"He knows what he means to me. I don't want anyone else." She placed the coffee mugs on the half empty platter of cookies and picked it up. "I've had a long day and there is nothing else I can show you. Mr. Sterling have a good trip home and enjoy the art you purchase from Ted. Ted, say hi to Naomi for me." She stood by the door and Lil opened it.

The two men took the hint and left.

Lil closed the door and shook her head. "That guy was slicker than snot from a crazed bull."

Ryan bounded down the stairs. "The gall of that guy, trying to get you to dump me for him."

Shandra laughed. It was the first time all day she'd felt the pressure of fear lifted. "You know I'd never go for such a slick talking guy."

He studied her. "Yeah, but he was dishing out the compliments like they were Tic Tacs."

She peered into his eyes. "He was only saying things you've told me."

"The difference is I meant it. He only said it to get you to fall for him."

"Grab that coffee pot and let's go in the house. I'm exhausted."

Lil opened the door again, and Shandra headed to the house. She heard Ryan behind her and Lil crunching across the cold surface toward the barn and her room.

At the house, Ryan opened the door.

Sheba pushed through ahead of her and bounded down the hall to the great room.

"I wish I was as happy-go-lucky as a dog," she said, carrying the platter into the kitchen.

Ryan put the coffee pot in the sink and swiped two cookies from the platter. "Yeah, never a care, only worrying when the next meal would be served and if someone in the house hears you when you want in."

She turned to him. "I take it he wasn't the man you thought he'd be?"

"I was glad he wasn't. A man bent on revenge can be dangerous." He wrapped his arms around her. "Let's get some sleep. Hopefully by morning, Whorter will have pulled more information out of PeeWee."

Yuletide Slaying

~*~

Shandra stood at the edge of a cliff. Ella's face appeared in the clouds.

"Why am I here?" She stared down into the deep gorge. Spotted colorful jagged objects that looked out of place were scattered across the bottom. She leaned out for a better look and her feet slid toward the edge. A hand reached out, grasping her coat and pulling her to safety. When she turned to thank the person, he was gone. She glanced back down into the gorge and saw half a leg and a boot. Her heart started beating and she screamed, "Ryan!"

"Shhh, I'm here."

Ryan's voice penetrated the fear bounding inside of her. She reached for him and clung to his solid form she knew so well.

"You had a dream." He held her in one arm and smoothed her hair away from her face with the other.

"Yes." She told him of the dream. "When I saw the leg, I thought…." She couldn't continue. The thought it had been Ryan at the bottom of the cliff had left her with the deepest grief she'd ever felt. "We have to figure out who is out to kill you. I don't want to lose you."

He held her close. "I'm not going anywhere. I'll call Oldham first thing in the morning."

She snuggled into his side, but sleep eluded her. Her mind spun in circles working through what they already knew. She had a feeling the little man the police arrested behind her barn wasn't the real killer.

Chapter Nineteen

Ryan crept out of bed at five. Shandra had had a rough night. He'd felt her tossing and turning long before she'd yelled his name and even after he'd tried to settle her down. Now, as dawn was breaking, she slept peacefully. He and Sheba sneaked out of the room, but he left the door slightly ajar in case she had more dreams.

He let the dog out and started the coffee pot brewing. In the great room, he snagged his laptop from the coffee table and picked up his phone. Two messages. He hit the icons and listened.

"We caught a kid putting a note in your parents' mailbox. It said you were in trouble and to meet you at South Tucker campground at midnight. After talking to the kid, he was paid fifty dollars to slip the note in the mailbox. State Police is sending a patrol car to check out the park."

He called his parents.

"Hello?" his mother answered.

"Mom, it's Ryan. Put the phone on speaker so Dad can hear me at the same time."

"You sound different. Did something happen?"

He heard the click of the speaker button being pushed and the familiar whirr of the refrigerator and beep of the microwave in the family kitchen.

"Since you refused to leave I had the police watching you. They caught someone putting a note in your mailbox last night. The note read like it was from me and I needed you to meet me somewhere. It was a fake. I would never send you a message. Any message coming from me would be through Shandra. If you get any phone calls or someone slips by the police, call Sheriff Oldham and tell him."

"Oh my! You shouldn't have to be worrying about us," his mother said.

"If dad wasn't so stubborn you could be on a tropical island right now and out of this mess," he said, knowing goading his dad wasn't going to make the old man change his mind.

"You need me and Conor here, not off getting a tan while your life is in danger."

He'd figured that would be his father's come back. "Call Conor, tell him not to believe anything unless it comes from Shandra and call the girls and let them know the same thing."

"Those scaredy-cat sons-in-law took·the girls and the grandkids and went into hiding," his dad said, not even hiding his disgust that they had fled.

"That's because I told them to. I don't want anyone

145

in the family harmed because of me." Exasperation seemed to always reach its peak when he talked to his dad.

"We'll tell them. You and Shandra be careful," Mom said.

"We will. Thanks, Mom. Stay home and don't bother the people there protecting you."

His dad humphed.

"We'll be fine. Take care."

The line went silent. He held the phone to his ear for a few more moments remembering the sound of his mom's voice and conjuring up the kitchen in the family farmhouse. He had wonderful memories of growing up there with his siblings. He'd be damned if he'd let some revenge-filled gang member take that away.

Back in the kitchen, he set the computer on the island, his phone beside it, and grabbed a cup of coffee. He had one person back in Chicago who might be able to shed some light on who was after him. If only his life was at stake, he wouldn't make the call, but whoever wanted him dead wanted him to suffer first. He'd not have his family or Shandra harmed to fulfill some sadistic S.O.B.s need to exact revenge.

He pulled out his wallet and dug under the flap in the cash section, pulling out a small piece of folded paper. Staring at the number a hundred memories flooded his mind. Most were good. He took a deep breath and tapped in the number.

"Shady Lady."

The sultry female voice laced with just the right amount of sugar, made him smile.

"Geena, it's Shawn O'Grady."

He was prepared for the phone to go dead. Instead,

he waited, listening to her breathing.

"So it's true. Word's been spreading you made it out of that hellish night alive."

"Months of rehab, but I'm alive. Word I hear, someone is out for revenge." He waited to see if she was willing to help. They'd had some good times. She'd helped him gather some information that brought the gangs down.

"The only one who is really steamed you're alive is Devin. He went nuts when his baby brother died that night." She blew out a breath. "I'm glad to hear you're still alive."

"I'm glad I'm still alive, too. Only Devin is out to get me?"

"Yeah. No one else seems to care. It was four years ago. These gangs change leadership so often no one remembers who the leader is half the time let alone who got killed four years ago."

"Except for Devin. Is he still in control of the south side?"

"Yeah, only he's added other real businesses to his resume. Besides dealing, he owns a clothing company and a resale outlet."

That meant he had more money and resources to pay for his revenge. He would need the FBI to lean on Moore. "Thanks, Geena. I hope your life is going well."

"It would be better if you hadn't been a cop…"

He knew she'd wanted more from him than what he could give back.

"What are you doing up so early?"

The husky voice behind him was the reason he couldn't give Geena all she'd wanted. He hadn't fallen for her like he had the sleep-tousled woman walking into the kitchen.

"It wasn't meant to be. Thank you for your help." He slid the phone to off and wrapped his arms around Shandra.

"Who were you talking to?" she asked, snuggling against him.

"An old friend from Chicago. Someone tried to lure mom and dad out to a campground last night on the pretense of helping me." It still irked him that someone had tried to put his family in danger.

She leaned back. "They're smart enough not to go."

"The police intercepted the note before my parents saw it. I told mom and dad the only person to believe anything about me is you."

Shandra relaxed in his arms and listened to the beating of Ryan's heart where her ear pressed to his chest. "I'm honored to be your spokesperson."

"My friend says only one gang even remembers what happened four years ago. Unfortunately, it is run by someone who lost a brother the night the gangs waged war on one another and the police."

Her heart beat with anticipation. "You know who is out to get you."

"I'm fairly certain. I have a few more inquiries to make."

"I'll make breakfast while you work."

"Woof!" Sheba barked at the back door.

Shandra let the dog in and returned to the kitchen to make breakfast. Ryan was already on the computer and phone at the same time. She caught tidbits of his conversation. He was catching whoever was on the other end of the conversation up with what he'd learned.

It bothered her that if he had someone to contact in Chicago, why he didn't do it sooner. The person couldn't have been a threat or he wouldn't have called him now.

She slid the plate with a cheese omelet under his nose and sat down beside him with a cup of tea and her own omelet. "Why did you pick now to call this person in Chicago?"

His body tensed. He shoved the computer up and pulled his breakfast in front of him.

He was stalling. His actions made it hard to swallow the bite she'd placed in her mouth.

"Because the woman had helped me get into the gangs."

"I see. And she wouldn't be happy to hear from you because…"

"I figured she'd be better off thinking I was dead just like everyone else." He spun his stool and grasped her hand. "When you're undercover, sometimes you have to do things that aren't who you really are. You take on a persona that will get you the information you need. It's exhausting to try and be someone you aren't twenty-four hours a day."

The desperation in his eyes, made her squeeze his hand, letting him know she wasn't judging him.

"Geena and I were dating. It was a good way to hang out in the pub she owned at all hours without it raising suspicion. Many members of the gang I was infiltrating spent many hours of the day and night at her pub."

"You were worried about calling her because you figured she'd pitch a fit."

His face reddened. "That's true. I didn't want to hurt her, but in the end, I was only using her. If she had feelings for me, I couldn't return them."

She leaned over and kissed his cheek. "You're a good man, Ryan Greer."

His phone buzzed. "Hold that thought." He picked up the phone and wandered into the other room.

Shandra finished her breakfast, cleaned up the mess, and headed to the bedroom to get dressed. She wanted to work on the new project today.

"That doesn't make sense," Ryan said when she came out of the bedroom dressed.

She lingered to hear more of the conversation.

"He conveniently came along and found the snowmobile running. No one gave it to him. I don't buy that. He's hiding something. He must be scared of the person who is really here to kill me. Which means he knows him or has met him." Ryan didn't say anything for a minute. "We have to figure out a way to make him talk. I'll be in Warner in two hours." He turned and found her watching him.

"Do you think you should be alone for two hours while driving to Warner?" She walked up to him. "Call Leeland and wait for him to ride with you."

"That will take too long." He picked up his computer and carried it into the great room, placing it on the dining table.

"Then I'll go with you." She headed to the back door for her boots.

"No. You're safer here," Ryan said, following her.

"You're safer here, too. But you won't stay and I won't let you go by yourself." She tugged on a boot with more force than usual, knocking her backward and into Ryan.

He caught her. "I don't want you in danger because of me. Stay here. If I'm not worrying about you it will be easier to do my job."

Shandra gave in, her mind spinning with how she could help.

"I'll text you when I get to the office." He shoved his feet into his boots, pulled on his coat, and kissed her. "See you tonight."

He opened the door, letting in big fluffy snowflakes. She hadn't even looked outside. The snow was coming down fast enough to cover Ryan's tracks to his SUV.

This could make her plan a bit trickier.

Chapter Twenty

"This ain't a good idea," Lil said, leaning against the Jeep's driver side door.

"I'm just running to town to flash this photo around. Someone had to have seen him talking to the person who killed the marshal and the local man." Shandra couldn't believe Lil was giving her such a hard time about going to town. "The snow has stopped. The weather report said we won't have more until right before Christmas."

The older woman glared at her. "It ain't the snow I'm worried about. You flashin' that photo everywhere is going to make you a target. I thought you were smarter than that."

"I'm only going to show it to locals. That won't get me into trouble." She grabbed the door handle. "Please move."

Yuletide Slaying

"That killer could be in the business when you're asking." Lil pressed her body even harder against the vehicle.

"I'll only ask when there aren't any customers. This is my chance to help Ryan and get this threat out of his life." Shandra grabbed her employee's arm and drew her away from the door. "I'm going. I'll be back by dark. Sheba, shotgun."

The big furry dog was more than happy to hop in and go for a ride.

"Besides, I need Chandler to check Sheba's stitches."

Lil snorted. "You do know that thing is a dog and not a human, don't you?"

"Yes." Shandra closed the door, started her Jeep, and drove out the barn door. She knew Lil would close the door and be waiting for her with all the lights on when she returned.

After Ryan had left, she'd opened his computer and printed a photo of the man they'd found with the missing snowmobile. She planned to show it around Huckleberry, since that was where she'd seen the man twice, and find out if anyone had noticed him with another person.

The drive to Huckleberry took longer due to the fact the county road leading to her place was always the last to be snowplowed after a snow storm. She met the plow headed out the road two miles before she reached town. Since it was still early for a lunch crowd at Ruthie's, she decided to go there first.

She parked in front of Dimensions Gallery. Inviting Naomi to go with her would give her friend a break from the gallery and give them a chance to visit.

Sheba whined, knowing they were at the gallery.

"Stay. I'm not going in, only getting Naomi."

Sheba's big brown eyes drooped even more at being left, but she laid down on the backseat.

Entering any art gallery soothed Shandra's senses. She enjoyed the way painters married colors and brought images to life. The solid bronze statues expressed each sculptor's sense of self and the world around them. Pottery was an ancient art and one she was proud to be sharing with the world. The way Ted and Naomi staged the pieces around one another showcased each one and complimented the others. It felt more like a much loved art piece in a home than waiting to be sold in a gallery.

"Shandra. What a wonderful surprise." Naomi's long legs carried her from the back of the gallery quickly.

"How about joining me for lunch? We didn't get to have any girl chat the other night." She rarely indulged in girl talk even with Naomi. She'd never had many female friends growing up. Hiding her heritage from friends was easier if she didn't have any close connections and living on a cattle ranch, she'd spent her non-school hours with the ranch hands.

"The men did monopolize the conversation." Naomi spun on her heel. "I'll get my coat and purse and tell Ted where I'm going. Hold on."

She took the time alone to wander to the section where her art was showcased. Her curiosity wanted to know which pieces Mick had purchased. A quick scan of the area revealed only two pieces missing. He'd talked about three. Oh well, two was better than none.

The click of Naomi's high-heeled boots grew near.

Yuletide Slaying

"Ted said you're working on something new. We have a couple blank spaces to fill." Her friend pulled on a down coat.

Shandra smiled. "I am working on something new. When it's done, you'll be the first gallery to see it." She headed to the door.

They fell in step and chatted about the colorful Christmas decorations and the morning's snow on the walk to the café.

"Two of my favorite customers," Ruthie said, her smile wide and welcoming when they entered.

Warm air accented with cinnamon and fresh bread wrapped around them.

"You made cinnamon rolls today." Shandra's mouth started watering at the enticing aroma.

"I did. Would you two like to share one?" Ruthie led them to the booth farthest from the door.

"I don't want to share," Naomi said, glancing at the pan of steaming rolls on the counter.

Ruthie and Shandra laughed.

"I'll get one for each of you." Ruthie laid menus on the table even though every local in town knew what was served at the diner.

"I'll have hot tea," Shandra said before the restaurant owner walked away.

"Me, too," chimed in Naomi.

They both shrugged out of their coats.

Ruthie returned with a tray carrying the two rolls and the tea.

"You didn't invite me here for girl talk," Naomi said, cutting into her cinnamon roll.

Shandra shook her head. "I'm curious about Mick Sterling." She slipped a bite of the cinnamon roll into

155

her mouth and savored the caramel frosting that Ruthie used on the rolls.

Naomi stopped the fork halfway to her mouth. "Is something wrong with you and Ryan?"

"No. I found Mick's paranoia interesting. You and I have never run into a buyer who was that paranoid about making sure the art was authentic. Made me wonder if he dealt in stolen art."

"His check cleared the bank today. We'll box up and ship the items he purchased tomorrow." Her friend leaned forward. "He was hard to pin down about his business."

Ruthie slid into the booth beside Shandra. "I could use a break." She had a cinnamon roll on a plate and a cup of coffee. "You learn anymore about the person who stabbed Sheba?"

"No. Have you seen the guy who ran off without paying?" Shandra knew Ruthie and her fiancé wouldn't allow the man back in the building without paying for what he'd already eaten.

"No. But Oscar over at the Quik Mart said he saw him hanging around behind the building. He yelled at him and he took off on a snowmobile." Ruthie's usual merry demeanor was frowning. "If the guy was down-on-his-luck, I would have fed him. But driving around on a snowmobile, that doesn't sound like he wouldn't have money for a meal."

Shandra tucked the information about the Quik Mart away. "The snowmobile isn't his."

Ruthie narrowed her eyes. "You know an awful lot about this guy. Give."

"He's part of the investigation into the man who ended up in the sleigh." That was all they'd get from her. No one but law enforcement was to know about the vendetta on Ryan.

The bell on the door jingled, heralding the start of the lunch crowd.

"It pays to have a cop for a boyfriend." Ruthie stood, gathering her plate with a half-eaten roll and her cup. "Looks like I need to get back to cooking."

Shandra nodded and dug into her cinnamon dessert.

"I think this is all I'll have for lunch." Naomi, leaned back, her plate as clean as if she'd washed it.

"Which pieces did Mick buy of mine?" Ever since her friend said they had waited for the check to clear to pack them, she'd wondered what he'd picked. He'd shown a liking for her first works while looking at the notebook.

"The two small water baskets and *Midnight Sun*." She picked up her cup. "He has a good eye."

He'd purchased three of her more traditional looking pieces. Any apprehension she'd had of him was slowly waning.

More people entered the diner.

"I need to get Sheba's stitches looked at. Thanks for having lunch with me." Shandra stood, slipping her coat on.

"I'm ready to go. I'll walk back with you." Naomi followed her to the counter.

They paid and exited, walking back to the gallery.

"I'm glad you asked me to lunch. Let me know when you'll be bringing in that new piece." Naomi gave her hug.

"I will." Shandra walked around to the driver's side of the Jeep and slid in behind the wheel.

Sheba met her with a wide, wet tongue.

"No kisses. We're going to go see Chandler then head over to the Quik Mart." She put the Jeep in gear and caught a glimpse of a man stepping back around the corner as she pulled away from the curb. It was an odd movement, unless he was backtracking to look at something that caught his attention in the window.

~*~

Ryan paced the hall in front of the room they used to interrogate suspects. "I can't believe PeeWee would rather go to jail for murder than tell us who is really behind this."

Agent Weatherly strode down the hall toward them. "It's confirmed he's part of Moore's gang. Most of the things he's been arrested for were jobs for Moore."

The information snapped Ryan out of his irritation. "Has anyone discovered if Moore is still in Chicago? I've seen him use a knife, he could have stuck the marshal and Perry." As much as he didn't want to think it was Devin Moore here to get revenge himself, he had a suspicion the gang leader was the one behind the killings.

"I have a man working on that. He was last seen in Chicago on Monday." Weatherly scrolled through messages on his phone.

"Both victims were killed before that." Ryan didn't like the thought there was a third person, or possibly a fourth or fifth. His gut twisted and gnawed. He'd downed too much coffee since arriving and no food. "I'm going to the diner." He headed for the door and found Leeland walking beside him.

"You hungry, too?" He knew better but asking

made it feel less like he was being babysat.

"Yeah. Craving one of those burgers the owner makes."

Ryan laughed. "Ruthie can sling as greasy a burger as anyone."

At the diner, Ruthie's waitress ushered them in. It was the tail end of the lunch rush.

Ruthie waved at him from the kitchen. "The usual?" she called out.

"Make it two. My friend hasn't lived until he's had one of your bacon cheeseburgers."

She gave him a thumbs up and went back to cooking.

"You know the cook pretty well." Leeland sipped the coffee the waitress brought him.

"She's friends with Shandra, and I tend to spend quite a bit of time in this town on cases lately."

The captain nodded. "The crime rate has risen here since they added more lifts and made the lodge a vacation destination geared toward the upper class. Before it had two runs and a small family setting to the lodge. I came here a few times as a teenager and skied."

"I did, too. The town and the ski lodge have definitely changed." He frowned. "And not for the better if you ask me."

Ruthie arrived with their burger baskets. "You missed Shandra. She and Naomi were in here before the rush."

He took his time replying, not wanting the panic or the anger that swirled in his mind to make him speak harshly. "Did she happen to say why she came to town?"

"To get Sheba's stitches looked at." Ruthie studied

him. "You aren't happy she's here. She is a grown woman you can't keep bubble wrap around." She tapped her toe as she talked.

The woman was one of Shandra's friends which meant she was as stubborn and independent as the woman he cared about.

"I know. She told me she was staying home. It took me by surprise that she was here." He didn't want to bet anyone that she wasn't only here to get the dog's stitches looked at. She was up to something that could get her hurt. He had no doubt.

Chapter Twenty-one

Shandra thanked Chandler for looking at Sheba as her phone buzzed. She glanced at her text messages and grinned. A text from Ryan. He wouldn't know she was in town if they text.

Her spirits dropped when she read the text.

You said you were staying home.

She felt the accusation clear to her toes. He knew she was in town. There was no use trying to pretend otherwise.

Sheba's wound was oozing. I wanted it checked.

Are you headed home now?

I have a stop to make.

Make it and go home, please. It's not safe for you to be out alone. We think there may be more people involved.

A shiver crept up her spine. More people. She

didn't like the odds.

I will. See you for dinner?

I'll try and I'll text if I won't make it.

K.

She started the Jeep and glanced all around. There was a blur around a corner again. Twice wasn't a coincidence. She put the vehicle in drive and headed to the Quik Mart.

Oscar was on duty at the gas pumps. Shandra eased up to the pumps and rolled her window down. Idaho was a pump-your-own gas state. Oscar owned the Quik Mart and felt it his duty to pump gas for the women and anyone who didn't want to get out and do it themselves. And his policy garnered him more business than the other station in town. Especially, during the winter months.

"Afternoon, Miss." Oscar touched the brim of his red cap with fold-down ear flaps. His bulbous nose was as red as his cap.

"Good afternoon, Oscar. Fill it up, please."

He went to work putting the nozzle in the tank. As was his way, he wandered back up to the open window. "Fair snow we had this morning."

"Yes. It was. I heard you chased off a man on a snowmobile the other day. It's surprising how people get around." She held her breath, hoping he'd take the bait. His talent was knowing everything that went on in Huckleberry.

"I sure did. That feller had been here twice before. He'd buy beer and snacks. But that day he was hanging around, making me nervous."

"Hanging around. Like waiting for someone?"

"Seen him talking to a man about ten minutes

before I run him off. Didn't want him loitering around to scare off customers." He nodded. The gas pump clunked, and he moved along the vehicle to the gas cap. After pulling the nozzle out, he punched buttons and brought her the slip.

"Was he talking to a local person?" She wanted to know more about the person PeeWee had talked with.

"Don't think so. Never seen him before and he got in a rental car with Washington plates." Oscar turned to go back in the store.

It was cold out and she didn't want to keep the old man out in the weather. She pulled forward, parked, and hurried into the store behind him. She picked up a pack of jerky and a bottle of water. At the counter, she smiled at the woman with cherry red hair, a nose piercing, and tattoos covering her left arm. Oscar's granddaughter.

Oscar filled a travel mug with coffee and sat in a chair by the door.

On her way out the door, Shandra stopped. "The out of state man. What did he look like?"

"He had a parka with the fur around the hood, jeans, and sport shoes."

"Did you get a look at his face?"

"Red hair, pointy chin. Don't usually pay that much attention but he was talking to that loiterer."

"Thank you, Oscar." She headed to the Jeep and climbed in.

Sheba smelled the jerky before she opened the package. Her large head pushed between the seats and rested on Shandra's shoulder, drool slid down the shoulder of her coat.

"Hold on, I have some for you." She held up a

piece and the dog covered it with her whole mouth.

The description Oscar had given her ran through her mind. *Do I dare call Ryan and tell him what I've discovered or wait until tonight?* She opted to tell him tonight. After his text message she had a feeling he wouldn't be happy knowing she'd played detective.

~*~

Shandra had a meal ready with all of Ryan's favorites. He'd yet to text he wasn't going to be home for dinner. She sat on the couch watching the flames in the electric fireplace and listening for him to arrive.

The blur of colors in the flames reminded her of the two times she'd thought someone had ducked around a corner. *Could that someone have had red hair?* She knew no one had followed her home. She'd made a brief stop at Jess Metcalf's for salad greens from his hot house. It was handy having a neighbor who enjoyed growing and selling produce. After turning, she'd sat in her Jeep for ten minutes before knocking on Jess's door. No one had gone by in that time.

Sheba sat up, her ears perked.

"Is Ryan here?" Shandra patted the dog's head and moved to look out the front window. Ryan's pickup came into view with his work SUV following behind.

Ryan parked the pickup in front of the barn, talked to whoever was in the SUV, and headed for the back door.

She stayed at the window, watching the SUV drive away. *Would the person actually leave or were they watching the house?*

"Smells good in here." Ryan appeared in the hallway.

"I'm glad you could come home." She met him in

the middle of the great room and accepted his embrace.

"There wasn't a reason to work any longer. Whorter and Weatherly are using all their resources to see if the head of the gang might be here." He released her, shifting an arm around her shoulders and leading her to the kitchen.

"Do you know what the guy looks like?" She held her breath.

"What do you know?" He spun her to face him. His hands gripped her shoulders.

"Oscar at the gas station said he'd chased off the loiterer with the snowmobile but he'd seen him talking to a man with a rental car and out of state license plates." She raised her gaze from his shirt to his eyes.

"What else."

"He said the guy had red hair and a pointy chin."

"Damn! He is here." He released her and pulled out his phone. He paced back and forth in the kitchen as she dished the dinner onto plates.

"Moore is here." He ran a hand across the back of his neck, a sure sign tension had built. "He's in a rental car." He stopped near her. "What state was the car from?"

"Oscar said Washington." She walked to the refrigerator and pulled out a beer. Ryan needed to unwind.

"Washington. Send someone to talk to Oscar at the Quik Mart. He saw Moore and the car. Then send people to all the motels. He has to be in one of them." He nodded. "Yes. I won't leave here until morning."

He shoved his phone back in the holder and stared into space.

Now was not the best time to tell him she thought

someone had been following her. Instead, she eased him onto the stool and put the beer bottle in his hand.

"Everyone is out looking for him. We're safe for now. Eat your dinner." She sat next to him.

"If it were any other gang leader, I know we'd get him or he would give up by now. But Devin Moore has finances to keep going. He's become a business man with contacts and money. And he was overprotective of his kid brother. The death has to be eating him up, because he gave in and allowed Dean to go to the alley that night."

His face contorted in pain and his gaze dulled.

She put her arms around him. "You were doing your job and were injured as well. You couldn't have stopped what happened."

He patted her hand. "But I've tried to change things in my mind every single night."

"The past is the past. There are things I'd like to change but it's impossible to do without a time machine." She kissed his cheek and straightened. "Eat."

Once he started eating, she talked about Sheba's antics while Chandler took the bandage off and checked out the wound.

Her phone jingled. She wasn't expecting a call from anyone. The number was Jess.

"Hello?"

"Shandra, this is Jess Metcalf. You know how we were talking about snowmobiles this afternoon? Well, I just heard one up on the mountain while me and the dogs were outside."

"How far away did it sound?" Ryan's body pressed to her back as he listened to the call.

"A mile maybe. At least on the other side of my

fence, I'd say."

"Thanks for calling." She slid her finger across the screen. "Did you hear all of that?"

Ryan eased back and shook his head.

"My neighbor, Jess, with the hot house, called to say he heard a snowmobile go by just now."

"How did he know you were interested in a snowmobile?" Ryan put his hands on the counter on either side of her and leaned in, his nose nearly touching hers.

"I stopped by there this afternoon to get the salad greens and happened to mention snowmobile tracks on my land." They'd talked of many things but she'd thrown that in knowing any snowmobile coming from town and staying off the road would have to go by his place.

"Happened to mention. Just like you happened to be talking to Oscar and he poured out all the information about the man in the out-of-state car."

She pushed on his chest, moving his face out of hers. "You should call in that bit of information."

He remained where he was. "Shandra, there is a reason I tell you to keep out of police business. It's to keep you safe."

"But I've come up with good information." She poked her finger in his chest. "Admit it, I have."

He growled. "That's not the point. The point is each time you snoop for information you put yourself in danger. I want you around for a long time. Let the professionals do their work."

"Would one of the 'professionals' have talked with Oscar or Jess? No. I happen to find out things because I go on with my life and see people."

Ryan shoved away from the counter and walked three steps away. He spun around and stalked back. "You can't continue to run all over the place alone. Moore wouldn't think twice about sticking you with a knife if he saw you. And for all we know there is someone else out there who wants me and you dead." His anger subsided and he grasped her arms. "I don't want to lose you. That's why I stayed instead of leaving and never seeing you again. Don't make me regret staying."

Tears burned in her eyes. She knew how he felt. The same gnawing fear she had in her stomach every time she knew he was headed into danger.

"I'm sorry. I'll stay here until you find the person." She threw her arms around him and hugged him tight.

His arms wrapped around her, holding her tight. "Thank you," he whispered and kissed her.

They remained locked in one another's arms for several minutes. He eased out of the embrace and reached for his phone. "I need to call in the snowmobile."

~*~

Shandra tossed and turned. She couldn't get to sleep knowing the person out to kill Ryan could be lurking in the woods outside. It was obvious Ryan trusted his co-workers. He slept. His arms and legs had been part of her problem of sleeping. He'd thrashed about the first hour after they went to bed. But now he was peacefully sleeping.

She slipped out of bed and padded quietly through the great room and into the kitchen. If she couldn't sleep she might as well make a cup of tea and work on some sketches.

168

The kettle started to whistle, and she pulled it off the stove. She added the kettle to a tray she'd put together and carried it into the great room. The light from the kitchen guided her to the chair in the sitting area by the patio doors. After placing the tray on the small side table she glanced out the glass doors and spotted what looked like a light bobbing through the trees.

Her heart landed in her throat. There was someone out in the trees. She watched the light gain in size. He was coming to the house.

She ran into the bedroom, tripping over Sheba and landing on the bed.

"What?" Ryan shot to a sitting position.

"It's me," she whispered. "There's a light coming toward the back of the house. From the woods."

"Stay put." He slipped out of bed and moved to the door. "Keep Sheba in here. Use my phone and call Whorter."

She nodded even though she knew he couldn't see it in the dark. He disappeared out the door, and she fumbled around on the side table until she found his phone. The light was bright when she turned the phone on. She shielded her eyes and scrolled through the contacts.

The phone rang several times.

"What's happening?" Whorter asked in a voice that sounded like he hadn't been asleep.

"This is Shandra. Ryan told me to call you. I saw a light bobbing in the trees behind my house. Ryan is investigating."

Whorter swore. "He knows better than to go out on his own. I'll send the men watching the road." The phone went silent.

It was a bit of a relief to know there had been officers watching out for them. But Ryan was all alone out in the woods.

She quickly dressed, ordered Sheba to stay in the room, and wandered out to the great room. She stared into the woods but didn't see any light. Ryan had told her to stay put. But he'd taken off out into the woods alone.

Her mind raced trying to decide what to do. Sheba barked and lights bounced in the front window. She peered out as two State Police officers burst out of the SUV.

Shandra flung the front door open. "I don't know where he is—" Her words were cut off by the blast of a rifle.

The men took off running around the side of the house. Shandra's heart stuttered in her chest.

Chapter Twenty-two

Ryan ripped the shotgun out of Lil's hands before she blew his head off. "What are you doing out here?"

"I heard a snowmobile and thought I'd come out and scare him off." She crossed her arms. "What are you doing out here?"

"Shandra saw your flashlight bobbing around in the trees and thought someone was coming to get us."

"Oh."

At least she had the common sense to see how she'd frightened her employer.

"Getting the person on the snowmobile is the job of the police, not you." He started back toward the house.

"Well, from what I've seen so far, they ain't doing a very good job at it." The crunch of the woman's boots following him revealed she wasn't going to be stubborn and continue hunting for the snowmobile unarmed.

Two men came crashing through the brush. A flashlight beam blinded him.

"What…" He put a hand up to ward off the light.

"We heard the shot."

He recognized State Trooper Taylor's voice. "It was Lil. She's trigger happy and probably scared away whoever might have been lurking in the woods."

The two men nodded and turned to walk back.

"Thanks for getting here so quick," he said, handing Lil's rifle back to her and stepping up alongside Taylor.

"Whorter told us to get our asses here," the other officer said.

He chuckled. "Shandra must have sounded convincing. I wish it had been the murderer. I'm getting tired of all these false leads."

"I'm tired of the police not doing their jobs," Lil piped up.

Taylor stopped.

Ryan grabbed his coat sleeve. "It's not worth arguing with her. Believe me, I know."

Shandra stood at the back door, her down coat on and her arms wrapped around her body as if she were holding herself together. She ran out and hugged him around the neck.

His heart raced at the relief he saw on her face. "I'm fine. Lil is a bit trigger happy but no one was hurt."

She released him and stared at Lil. "What were you doing out there?"

"I heard the snowmobile and thought I'd take care of the trespasser once and for all. Police can't seem to do it."

Lil's indignant tone made Ryan smile. He'd come to learn the woman was more bark than bite. And not happy if she didn't have something to complain about.

"Everyone come in. I have hot chocolate and coffee." Shandra ushered everyone into the kitchen.

"I need to call this in," Taylor said, and wandered into the other room to make his call.

Ryan held out his hand to the other officer. "Ryan Greer, detective with the Weippe County Police."

"James Decker." He shook hands. "I've never been involved with this kind of a man hunt before."

"I'm glad you came so fast," Shandra said, handing the man a cup of coffee.

"We were sitting out on the county road. Whorter has a car on this road twenty-four seven until we catch this guy." He sipped the coffee.

Taylor returned to the kitchen. "Whorter is happy it was a false alarm but also exasperated we haven't caught the guy." He took the cup of coffee Shandra offered him.

Lil stood her shotgun in the corner of the laundry room and slid onto a stool. Shandra placed a cup of hot chocolate in front of her.

Ryan sat next to the bristly woman. "How long ago did you hear the snowmobile and how far away did it sound?"

She yanked the stocking cap off her head and ran a hand through her short white hair, standing it up like spikes. "I heard the sound about one. Dressed and went out into the woods to find the trespasser. I could still hear the purr of the engine. Like it was idlin'." She sipped the chocolate. "I followed the sound and just as I thought I was getting close, it took off." Her hand smacked the counter. "I found the tracks and where it had been sitting."

"How far away? Which direction did it go?" Ryan had a feeling he knew the direction it went. The vacant residence next door.

"I'd walked about a mile when I came to the tracks. He went toward the old Randal place."

Ryan nodded and turned his attention to the two staters. "You need to go see if anyone is staying in the place a mile east of here. I thought someone had checked, but if the person out there tonight is headed that direction that has to be where he is staying."

The two officers guzzled the coffee and headed out the back door.

Shandra stared after the two state police officers and asked the question that had been rattling in her head ever since Lil mentioned a snowmobile. "I thought you had the guy riding the snowmobile locked up."

"We do." Ryan sipped the hot chocolate she'd put in front of him.

"Then who is riding on my property now?"

He put the mug down and faced her. "Possibly the person working with PeeWee." He glanced at Lil and sighed. "PeeWee swears up and down he didn't kill anyone. But he knows who did and is more scared of that person than he is of going to jail for murder."

She shivered even though she still wore her coat. There were too many unknowns about all of this. The only thing they truly did know was two people had been killed in the same way and one of them was here to warn Ryan.

"Go sit by the fire. I'll clean up and come sit with you." Ryan started cleaning the kitchen and Lil slid off the stool.

She picked up her rifle and slipped out the back door before Shanda had walked into the great room.

Sheba whined and knocked on the bedroom door. She crossed the room and shoved on the door. The dog burst through the door as soon as her head fit through. The weight of the dog shoving the door, sent Shandra careening into the room.

"What's a matter girl?" Ryan asked in the kitchen. Moments later the back door opened and shut. Apparently, Sheba had needed to go outside in a hurry.

Shandra regained her balance and curled up on the end of the couch nearest the fireplace. *Grandmother come to me. We need to get this sorted out*. She closed her eyes, slowed her breathing, and willed herself to relax and nod off.

Two men fought on the edge of the cliff she'd been at before in her dreams. The one had red hair and a pointy chin. The rest of his features were fuzzy. The other man was tall, broad shouldered, and had dark hair. Her heart started to stammer when she really looked at him and realized it wasn't Ryan. But who? She tried to walk toward them but it was as if a glass wall stood between them. She could press her nose up against it and see, but couldn't move forward. "Ella, what does this mean?"

Grandmother stood beside her. She waved to the men and then to a hand clinging to the top of the cliff. Instinctively, she knew who that hand belonged to. "Ryan!" She kicked and beat on the glass keeping her prisoner.

"Shandra. I'm here. Wake up, it's just a dream." Strong arms banded around her, holding her to a

175

wide chest. She pressed her ear against him and listened to his rapidly beating heart. Ryan's woodsy aftershave filled her nostrils. He was alive and here with her.

"You're shaking. Was your grandmother in the dream?" He kissed the top of her head and held her tight.

"Yes." She told him of the dream and the part of him hanging onto the side of the cliff.

"Nothing's going to happen to me. You heard Taylor say they have someone on the road all the time."

"But not the woods. They keep traveling through my property on snowmobiles without a care." She pushed out of his arms and sat up. "I'm getting tired of them using my land as if it's a freeway."

"We're working on bringing in our own snowmobiles to keep an eye on the fence lines." He stood, dragging her to her feet as well. "There's only a few more hours left until I need to get up. Let's get some sleep."

She followed him into bed, but once again tossed and turned until sleep finally tugged her under.

Grandmother appeared again. She pointed to the bottom of the cliff. Shandra shook her head, her heart racing, and backed away from the edge. Ella grasped her hand, leading her to the edge. She didn't want to look. To see Ryan at the bottom of the canyon, but Grandmother insisted she look. She opened one eye and peeked.

There wasn't a body.

What was she missing? She scanned the side of the cliff all the way to the bottom. There was a small pile of what appeared to be pottery. "I don't understand," she said. Grandmother disappeared without answering.

Chapter Twenty-three

Ryan rose, let himself out of the bedroom along with Sheba, and headed to the kitchen for a cup of coffee and a phone call.

He opened the back door and the big, goofy dog bounded outside. After the coffee machine started perking, he pulled out his phone and dialed.

"Whorter."

"Greer. Did the two staters who were here last night find anyone at the house up the road?" He leaned against the island, watching the coffee drip into a cup.

"They found fresh vehicle tracks. A padlock was on the shed out back. They couldn't look in there without a warrant."

"You're getting one this morning." He had to know if that was where the suspects were hiding. "Did any of the officers asking at the hotels and motels find Moore?"

"I have a call into Judge Hilton for the warrant and

there isn't a man fitting Moore's description registered at any of the hotels or motels. Not even the ski resort," the state detective added.

"He's here. Has anyone seen his car? The rental from Washington." A person from Chicago with no ties to the area had to be staying where they'd find him. "What about bed and breakfast places?"

"I'll have someone working on that this morning."

Ryan picked up the full cup of coffee and sipped. "I'll stay at Shandra's until you have something to move on."

"You're not planning on checking out the neighbor on your own." Whorter's tone held a threat.

"No. If I stay here, I know Shandra won't be out digging up information and getting herself in deeper."

Whorter chuckled. "That one is a handful. Good luck."

He'd find humor in it, too, if they'd been talking about someone else's woman.

Sheba barked at the back door.

He let her in and glanced around outside. He'd brought fear to Shandra's life. And instead of fleeing, she ran head-on into the mess.

"Good, you're still here," Shandra said from the kitchen doorway.

"I'm not going anywhere unless I get a call they've found the suspect." He hooked a mug from the cabinet and poured steaming water from the kettle he'd set to heating when he'd started the coffee.

"They didn't find anyone at the Randal's?"

"Not yet. They did find a padlocked outbuilding. Whorter is working on a warrant to check that."

Her brow furrowed. "I don't understand how an

178

outsider can stay hidden so well."

His same reaction. "We're overlooking something…" He ran back through all they knew so far.

"Has anyone checked to see if there is a relative that could be keeping him?" She brightened. "Some place near a cliff."

"Why a cliff?" He handed her the mug of tea.

"There's been a cliff in the last three dreams I've had." She didn't look at him.

"What else has been in the dreams? You haven't been telling me everything." He stood in front of her, tipping her chin up so her eyes gazed into his.

She audibly gulped. Her eyes glistened with tears.

"It can't be that bad," he said, hating the fear he saw in her eyes.

"Y-you've been in trouble."

"We already know this person is out for my blood. That's not new." He had to be flippant about someone out to kill him. If he showed fear, Shandra would go into protector mode. He didn't need or want her getting hurt on his account.

She set her mug down and spun to the refrigerator. "I'll make breakfast."

He conceded to give her space. "I'm going to check on the possibility of Moore having family here."

The minute Ryan stepped out of the kitchen, Shandra dropped her face into her hands, covering the tears trickling down her cheeks. They had to find these people before they settled their score with Ryan.

~*~

It was nearing noon when Ryan's phone buzzed. He checked the caller.

Leeland. The text read. *Pick you up in ten minutes.*

He put down the book he'd been reading and glanced over at Shandra. She'd fallen asleep thirty minutes after sitting down to work on sketches. All her tossing and turning the night before had caught up to her.

She looked so peaceful he hated waking her, but she'd be mad if she woke and he was gone. He crossed the room and kissed her forehead. "Shandra. Honey, wake up."

She stirred, murmuring his name.

"Yes, it's Ryan. Leeland is coming to pick me up." He kissed her cheek. "I'll be back by dark."

Her head bobbed as if she heard him.

He was pretty sure she wasn't going to remember this conversation. A slip of paper lay on the coffee table. Using the pencil from her hand, he left a note.

At the back door, he put on his outdoor clothing. Sheba had followed him into the room.

"Stay. You were out not that long ago."

She sat but gave him a dissatisfied look.

Outside, he headed for the barn. Lil needed to know he was leaving. She'd keep watch for any strangers.

He rounded the back of the barn and entered through the door by the tack room, also Lil's domain. All the lights blazed in the main section of the barn.

The crusty older woman crouched by the front leg of her old mare, Sunshine. She crooned sweet nothings to the horse as she rubbed a liniment on the animal's leg.

"Lil."

She jolted and came to her feet. "What are you doin' sneaking up on a person?"

"I wasn't sneaking. I'm going out with Captain Leeland. I told Shandra, but she wasn't completely awake. I also left her a note." He waved at hand at the shotgun leaning up against the stall. "Keep an eye out for strangers."

"Will do. Don't want nothin' to happen to Shandra." She wiped the liniment from her hand and walked out of the stall.

"If you hear a snowmobile, call me. Don't go off into the woods. I don't want Shandra left alone for any reason." He had to make it clear to the woman, Shandra could be in danger.

"I ain't goin' nowhere. Get." She waved him away and picked up the shotgun.

Satisfied she would watch over Shandra, he left the barn by the man door in the front. A dark SUV came into view up the driveway.

He met the vehicle before Sheba might hear it and bark.

Inside, he glanced over at Leeland. "How many are going with us?"

"Four staters and the FBI agent."

Seven was a good number if they came across the suspect hiding in the outbuilding. He'd spent a good deal of the morning trying to find a family connection in Idaho to Moore. He came up with nothing. He'd even tried PeeWee and couldn't find any connection. The Randal property was the logical place for them to be staying. It was empty and close to Shandra's.

They didn't say anything else the ten minutes it took to reach the driveway and pull up behind the two state rigs and a dark unmarked SUV.

Everyone stepped out of the vehicles at the same

time, converging in the middle beside Weatherly's SUV.

"The warrant is for any building on the premise. We'll start with the padlocked building and then check out the others," Weatherly said.

They nodded and headed to the smaller building beside the barn. It appeared to be a storage shed for gardening tools from the empty flower pots and hoses against one side.

One of the staters snapped the padlock with bolt cutters. Weatherly grabbed the handle and pulled.

Empty. No one was hiding inside. But there was a cloth grocery bag on a bench. Ryan reached over to see where the bag came from and three mice ran out a hole in the bottom. A riddled bread sack and mouse droppings covered the bottom of the sack around a jar of peanut butter.

"Someone is feeding the mice," he said, dropping the bag back to the bench. A pile of tarps had blankets spread over them. "Someone has been staying in here."

Leeland pointed to one of the State Policemen. "If there's a smooth spot check for prints."

"Has anyone checked the barn lately?" Ryan asked.

"No." Weatherly headed out of the small building and straight to the barn. He swung the big door in the front open, allowing light to filter into the open area of stalls.

Ryan found a light switch to the side of the door and flicked it on.

There wasn't a nook or cranny that wasn't lit up.

"Why do you think someone was staying in the small building and not this one?" Weatherly waved his hand. "It's better insulated than the shed."

"Maybe he figured with a padlock on the building no one here looking to buy the place would know he was staying there." Ryan backed out of the barn and headed to the house. He'd been in the house when Mr. Randal was killed. It was huge, and costly. He remembered there had been an alarm system.

"The Huckleberry Police would know if someone had broken in here. I would think the real estate agent in charge would have kept the alarm system activated given how isolated this is." He stood on the porch. "But check all the windows on the ground floor anyway."

The three state policemen set out checking the perimeter of the house.

"Where's the snowmobile?" he stared at the buildings.

"We confiscated the snowmobile PeeWee was riding when we caught him." Leeland's look said he wondered if Ryan was thinking straight.

"Not that one. The one Lil heard last night. The one someone rode here and then left in a car." He turned to Weatherly. "I was told the state police who left Shandra's came here and said it looked like a car had left here recently." He waved his arms. "That snowmobile."

~*~

Shandra woke and rubbed her stiff neck. Falling asleep on the couch always left a kink in some part of her body. Sheba shoved her muzzle into her lap and whined.

"You want out?"

The big slobbery mouth opened and woofed.

She shoved to her feet and down the hall to let Sheba out the back door. The clock on the microwave blinked a white 2:00. She'd slept four hours. The two cups sitting on the island jogged her memory. Ryan.

He said he wasn't going anywhere. She made a cup of tea and returned to the living room. A piece of paper lay on the floor. Sheba's tail must have brushed it off the table.

Shandra, I tried to wake you. Leeland picked me up to check out the old Randal place. I'll be back soon. Ryan

When did he leave? Her stomach growled.

Back in the kitchen, she opened the dishwasher. He had to have left before lunch because there were only the dishes from breakfast in the machine. How long did it take to search the Randal place?

The back door opened and Lil stomped in.

"I figured you were up when I saw Sheba loping into the trees." She propped her shotgun in the laundry room and plopped down on a stool.

Shandra had a feeling Lil liked the excuse to carry her shotgun everywhere she went. "Have you had lunch?"

"Yeah. But I'll take a couple cookies if you want someone to eat with you."

She filled a cup with the coffee Ryan had made that morning and popped it in the microwave. "When did Ryan leave?"

"About ten-thirty or eleven." Lil picked up a cookie and bit.

"He's been gone a long time." She strode into the other room and picked up her phone. No messages.

"I suppose a big house like that would take a while to look through." Lil slid off the stool and grabbed the coffee out of the microwave.

"Hmmm…" Shandra spread peanut butter on two slices of bread and bit into it. "Can you think of any place someone might be staying around here that they wouldn't have to sign in or give their name?"

"The nondenominational church has a couple of rooms in the back. I stayed there a time or two when I was kicked from here." The older woman pulled her stocking cap off. "They don't ask who you are. They give you a bed and offer a mid-day meal if you want."

Shandra washed down a bite of the sandwich with tea and picked up a pen and notepad. She wrote, *church*, on the pad. "Anywhere else?"

"Mrs. Ellard rents out rooms. If you pay cash she doesn't ask any questions." Lil picked up another cookie.

She scribbled Ellard on the pad and picked up her phone. This was a good excuse to see where Ryan was and what he'd found out.

"You woke up," he answered his phone.

"Yes. What did you find out at the Randal's?" She tapped the notepad with the pen, hoping they'd caught someone.

"Someone had been staying there. I think PeeWee from the way things looked. We're spread out through the trees behind the buildings looking for the snowmobile everyone heard last night."

A shout rang out in the distance.

"I think someone found it."

"Before you hang up. I asked Lil about other places to stay that weren't motels. She said the nondenominational church has a few rooms and Mrs. Ellard rents rooms. You might check there."

"Church and Ellard." He was puffing as he spoke.

185

"We'll check those when we leave here. Don't wait up for me."

"Be careful."

"I will."

The line went silent. She put the phone down and picked up her mug of tea.

Lil stared at her. "What did he say?"

"They're going to check out those two places." She sipped her tea and stared out the window at the growing dusk. Winter days were so short. "I think I'll work in the studio for a while."

"I'm going to check on Sunshine and I'll come take those coasters out of the kiln." Lil picked her shotgun up as she left the house.

Seeing her employee packing a shotgun around didn't help her creative muse, but she needed to stay busy to not worry about Ryan and what he might find.

Chapter Twenty-four

Ryan was still chilled to the bone from traipsing around in the woods looking for the snowmobile. But they'd found one and discovered it was stolen. Now he and Leeland were headed to the church to see if Moore was staying there.

He was thankful Shandra had relayed the information to him and not headed out on her own to check it out. It was a sign she was learning to trust and accept he knew what was best for her safety.

Leeland pulled into the nondenominational church parking lot. The long low building was a good size. There were only two churches in town. This one catered to all the religions other than Catholic and Mormon. There was a small Catholic church on the other side of town and the Mormons traveled to Warner to worship. Each denomination had a service time written on the sign out front. That was why the church was well taken care of. The various religions helped to keep the building maintained.

They entered the unlocked front doors and walked down between the pews toward a small stage with a pulpit and a large wooden cross. The building was otherwise plain by church standards. No stained glass scenes or shrine or any embellishment.

"Do you know if anyone stays here that can answer questions?" Leeland asked, stopping in front of the pulpit.

Ryan shrugged. "I haven't dealt with anyone from here." He spun in a slow circle and decided to check the door to the right of the stage. He turned the knob and entered a small room with a desk and many books on two floor to ceiling bookshelves. There was a small door on the other side of the room. He opened that door and found a hallway with doors on either side.

Voices carried down the hall and light glowed at the end. He continued and walked into a large room filled with tables and chairs. Two women and a man sat at a table. They looked up as they approached.

"Hi. I'm Detective Greer and this is Captain Leeland with the Weippe County Sheriff's Office."

The women's gazes dropped to the table and the man glared.

"Hello, I'm Rick Johnson, the in-residence minister. Can I help you?" A man of about fifty stepped out of what appeared to be a kitchen. He was dressed in slacks and a navy blue sweater with a white shirt collar sticking out the neck of the sweater.

"I'm Detective—"

"I heard who you were," Mr. Johnson cut in.

"Follow me to my office. I don't want you upsetting the guests." He led the way back down the hall to the small office.

Once they were all in the room he closed the door. "What is this about?"

"We're looking for this man." Leeland held a photo of Devin Moore up for the man to see.

"He's not here. I haven't seen him at the weekly meal either." He looked up from the photo. "What has he done?"

"We aren't at liberty to say. If you do see him, please call." Ryan handed him a card. This place was a strike out.

He and Leeland returned to the SUV. "Looks like we're headed to Mrs. Ellard's." He rattled off the address, noting it was on the north side of town.

Ten minutes later they turned a corner and drove into a residential area he'd only been called to once. A neighbor had insisted someone had stolen his lawn mower. Turned out his wife had taken it to be worked on without his knowledge.

"I like these older houses. They have more character than the new ones on the west side of town." He'd always been partial to the older homes.

"This is the old part of Huckleberry. There was a narrow gauge railroad through here in the early nineteen hundreds. That's how the town first started. They needed water and wood to fuel the engines between Missoula and Coeur d'Alene." Leeland grinned. "My Julie is a history nut. Every once in a while, what she tells me sticks."

Ryan laughed. He knew what the captain was talking about. He'd come to know more about pottery than he'd ever had an inkling of knowing from listening to Shandra when she didn't think he was listening.

He pointed. "That one on the end, the two-story with the blue trim, that's Mrs. Ellard's."

Leeland pulled up on the opposite side of the street. They checked the two cars in the driveway. Neither one had out-of-state plates.

Ryan stepped out and headed across the street with Leeland on his heels. He knocked on the door and scanned the porch spanning the length of the front of the house. "Mrs. Ellard does a nice job of keeping this place up."

The door opened.

A tall thin woman in her seventies stood on the other side of the screen door. "May I help you?"

Leeland introduced them and stated why they were there. "Do you have a renter by the name of Devin Moore staying here?"

She shook her head. "There's a Kevin." She smiled. "He's a nice boy."

"Does Kevin look like this?" Ryan showed her the photo of Moore.

"Yes. That's Kevin." Her gaze latched onto Ryan's face. "He's a good boy. Why would you want to talk to him?"

"We can't tell you at this time. Is he here?" Ryan peered beyond the woman into the house.

"No, he and his friend went out a couple hours ago." Her voice wobbled a bit.

He understood her fear. She was an elderly woman who took strangers in. Knowing she had someone the police were looking for living in her home had to make her anxious.

"We'd like to search his room," Leeland said, grasping the handle on the screen door.

"Oh, I don't think you should. I mean, I pride myself on not butting into my renters' lives or their things."

"Ma'am, this person may have killed a U.S. Deputy Marshal and a local man. We need to discover what we can about him and wait for him to return." Leeland pulled the door open and stepped inside.

Ryan followed, taking hold of Mrs. Ellard's boney elbow and guiding her into the house.

Shandra arched her back, easing the tense muscles from hunching over the pot she'd been crafting the last five hours. It was finished, all but the handles she'd apply tomorrow. She stood and stepped back. A smiled tipped her lips and her heart sang. This was just the beginning. She could envision a whole series of vases in different sizes, glazed and unglazed using this rope technique.

By the time she cleaned up the clay, covered the vase, and turned out the lights, it was closing in on midnight. She glanced up at the bright twinkling stars in the dark blue sky. The quarter moon put out little light but what it did was magnified by the brilliant white snow. Walking from the studio to the house would have been easy even if the Christmas lights on the buildings weren't glowing.

She headed straight for the shower. The hot water pulsing on her back eased the strain of working without getting up and moving around for hours. Out of the shower, she dressed in sweats and slipped her feet into her favorite fluffy slippers. She made hot chocolate and filled a plate with cheese and crackers.

With the plate balanced on her phone in one hand and hot chocolate in the other she sat down on the couch to wind down.

Sheba gave a muffled bark at the back door. She'd taken off out of the studio the minute Shandra had opened the door.

"Coming!" She strode down the hall and opened the door. Her gaze fell on what Sheba had in her mouth.

She caught hold of the stocking cap in Sheba's mouth. "Let go."

The dog released the garment.

"Where did you get this?" It was a full face cap. The kind a snowmobiler or skier might wear. She stared into the woods beyond the buildings. Tingling at the base of her neck set her stomach churning. Was someone out there watching them right now? Had Sheba taken this from someone or had she found it?

"In!" She shut the door behind the dog and turned the deadbolt. After tossing the cap onto the drier, she strode to the great room and her phone. She held the cell in her hand trying to decide if Sheba finding a ski cap warranted calling Ryan. It could have fallen out of one of the search and rescue volunteers' pockets. It was ridiculous to call Ryan.

Her finger still hovered over the screen.

"No! I won't call him. It's ridiculous to think you took it from someone. You're scared of your own shadow." She rubbed Sheba's ears and settled back on the couch to enjoy her cheese, crackers, and hot chocolate.

~*~

A jazz tune woke Shandra. She blinked and

grabbed for her phone sitting on the coffee table. She didn't recognize the number.

"Hello?"

"S-shandra, it's Miranda. Miranda Aducci."

The woman's voice sounded strained.

"What's wrong?" She glanced at the mantle clock. 2:15.

"I-he…" Sobs cut off the words.

"Miranda, where are you? What happened?" Her chest squeezed and she willed her friend to offer more information.

"I'm at Maxine's. I-he…" She sniffed and she groaned. "Please come."

"Where's Maxine?" She didn't like the fear in Miranda's voice. The word "he" rang out in Shandra's mind. Some man had assaulted her friend.

"She's busy. Cl-cleaning up. Could you come, please?"

"Call the police. I'll be there as soon as I can get there." She pulled the phone away from her ear and heard.

"No! Please, stay on the phone."

"Miranda, I'm coming, but you need to call the police." She hurried to the bedroom and kicked off her slippers, shoving her feet into her fur-lined boots she only wore on special occasions. The quiet on the other end of the call made her nervous. "Are you still there?"

"Y-yes. I-I can't call the police. I don't want anyone. Please, don't tell anyone."

Miranda's pleas speared her heart. She knew what it was like to feel vulnerable after a man had harmed you.

"I won't. But I need to hang up so I can get the

Jeep out and get to you. I'll call you when I'm about to town. Okay?"

Sniffing resounded over the phone. "Okay. Hurry."

"I will."

She ran to the back door, pulling on her coat and grabbing her purse. She shoved her phone in her coat pocket.

Sheba whined behind her.

"Sorry girl, you need to stay." She patted the big broad head and closed the door, locking it behind her.

She flung the barn doors open and hopped in the Jeep.

Lil appeared at her side window, startling her.

"Shoot, Lil, you nearly gave me a heart attacked," she said, rolling down the Jeep window.

"Where are you going? It's purt near three in the morning."

"My friend Miranda called. She's been hurt. I'm going to her." She waved her hand. "Move and close the doors behind me."

"Where is she?" Lil asked, backing away.

"Maxine's." She shoved on the throttle, burst out of the barn, and fishtailed across the packed snow and into the plowed drive. Her speed was too fast for the conditions, but she had an urgent need to get to Miranda and soothe the young woman. What man in his right mind would harm her? She was an imposing woman at six foot and a little over two hundred pounds. It would have taken a large man to overpower her.

The county road was empty this time of night, she kept to the middle of the road and sped into town in thirty minutes. A record for her even in summer weather. She slowed down once she turned onto the main street. If she sped and the local cop stopped her it would slow her getting to Miranda and she would have to tell him where she was going.

She turned down the side street beside Dimensions Gallery and continued past Maxie's Bar. She did a U-turn and parked in front of the bar. It was dark inside. A glance upwards showed lights on in the apartment above the bar, where the owner Maxine lived.

Instead of pushing through the front doors, which she figured would be locked, she walked to the alley side of the bar and up the stairs on the outside of the building. At the top, she knocked.

No one called out.

She tried the door. The knob turned and she pushed.

Miranda sat in a chair, her hair draped across one side of her face. Her head shook violently and Shandra saw the rag stuffed in her mouth and bruises on her cheek.

Before she could spin and dive for the stairs, a strong arm came out from behind the door, grabbing her and throwing her against the wall as the door slammed shut.

Chapter Twenty-five

Shandra stared into dark blue eyes that showed no emotion. He wore a ski cap like the one Sheba had brought home. She reached up to get a handful of the cap.

He reacted faster, grasping her arm and wrenching it behind her. With quick movements, he taped her wrists together behind her back.

She tried to stomp on his toes and found herself up on his shoulder like a sack of grain.

The red-haired man Ryan said was out to kill him walked out of what appeared to be a bedroom. "We have the bait," he said in a satisfied tone.

"Ryan won't come for me. We had a fight and he left." It was all a lie but she'd lie to the devil if it kept Ryan alive.

The man laughed. "I'm not a fool. We've watched

enough of you two together to know he'll show up when we call." He motioned to Miranda. "We'll take her. Can't leave any witnesses."

"No!" Shandra shouted and kicked her feet at the man holding her on his shoulder.

"Legs." The man holding her barked.

Rough hands wrapped something around her legs from her knees down.

"That should keep her from going anywhere."

"The police around here aren't dumb. They'll find you." She stopped as the man ran a length of tape over her mouth.

"I'll bring the car into the alley." The red-headed man, Devine Moore, left the apartment and the other man dumped her onto the couch.

She scanned the room looking for signs of Maxine. Where was the woman? Had she been harmed as well? Her gaze fell on Miranda. The young woman appeared to be in shock. Her hands were taped behind her back, and her feet were taped in front of her. But her eyes weren't covered. Did she know who the man in the ski mask was? It was obvious he didn't want her to recognize him. But what of Miranda? Had she seen his face? Did that mean… A shudder rippled through her body at the thought she might be spared and Miranda not.

"Let's go." Devin burst through the door. "You take the big one, I'll get this one." He walked up to her, his eyes wild.

"Wait." The masked man tied a scarf around her eyes.

Which meant he was taking his mask off.

Space and momentum were exaggerated as her

body was lifted and flung over a shoulder. She couldn't stop her head from bumping into the man's back or his hand from feeling her thigh through her sweats. She squirmed but stopped as soon as she felt him dropping down each step. She didn't want a fall to kill her. But she could make his getting her into the car hard and possibly make enough noise to rouse someone. It was early morning. There had to be someone prowling the alley. Maybe Mark from the donut shop.

When she registered he walked on flat ground, she started swaying her body back and forth hoping to kick something and make noise. She did manage to hit something with her feet that sounded like a metal trash can. She tried to picture the alley in her mind. She didn't remember seeing one on her visits to Ted and Naomi.

The back of her head hit the car as the man dumped her into a seat. He shoved her legs in and the door closed. She worked at sitting up, but felt weight on the other side of her and the car bounce. Another door closed and then two more.

The car started up and moved.

She used her head to try and touch Miranda. To let the woman know she wasn't alone with the men.

"Down!" said the man in the ski mask. Rough hands shoved her down. Miranda's body was forced on top of her.

~*~

Ryan stared at his watch. Six. They'd waited at the Ellard place all night. Moore was a no-show. Two state police out of uniform and in an unmarked car were taking over.

"How about a donut and some coffee before I take

you home?" Leeland asked as they pulled away from the curb.

"Sounds good. I can get a dozen to take to Shandra." He twisted his neck right and left. It had been a while since he'd pulled an all-night stake-out. His head turned to the right in time to catch a glimpse of copper. "Turn at the next street and head west on Pine."

Leeland glanced over at him but did as he asked.

Sure enough. Shandra's Jeep was parked in front of Maxie's. "Stop."

He hopped out and tried the doors. They weren't locked. He shook the doors on the bar but they were locked. His phone buzzed. A glance at the name froze his heart.

"Lil, where's Shandra?" he ordered.

"She got a call from Miranda saying she was at Maxine's. But she left three hours ago and she's not answering her phone." Lil sounded as frustrated as he did.

"I'll let you know if I find her." He hung up and strode down the alley to the stairs leading up to the apartment above.

"What's wrong?" Leeland asked on his heels.

"Shandra had a call from a friend to come here." He knocked on the door. Nothing. He grabbed the knob and turned. Stepping back, he pulled out his Glock and motioned to Leeland he was going in. The captain nodded, his Glock in his hands.

Ryan eased the door opened and scanned what he could see. Nothing. He pointed to the kitchen and moved toward the only other door in the place. A shove opened the door and he spotted Maxine struggling with the tape holding her arms and legs together.

"Maxine, it's Detective Ryan Greer." He moved to the bed and pulled out his knife.

She stopped struggling and he shoved the scarf off her eyes and pulled the tape off her mouth.

"Ow! When I get my hands on the son-of-a-bitch who did this."

He cut the tape and grasped her shoulders as Leeland entered the room. "Who did this? Where's Shandra?"

"Shandra? They burst in here with Miranda. Looked like one of them had hit her."

"Who was it?"

"I'd never seen the red-headed guy before. The other one wore a ski mask." She rubbed her wrists. "You think they have Shandra?"

"Lil said Shandra got a call last night from Miranda to meet her here." Ryan didn't understand how Miranda fit into all of this. Had she been dragged in as bait for Shandra? Moore and his accomplice must have followed her enough to know her haunts and friends.

"I heard voices out there but I couldn't get loose." She stood up. "Don't stand here looking dopey, go find them and get Shandra and Miranda safe." She flapped her arms like a goose getting ready to take off in flight.

Ryan shoved his knife into the sheath and strode out of the apartment and down the steps. Ted stood outside the back door to the gallery.

"Did you see or hear anything in the alley last night?" he asked the gallery owner.

"I heard car doors slam about four this morning. That was after I heard another noise that woke me."

"Did you look out? See anything?" Ryan was grasping at whatever he could to figure out where

Moore could have taken the women.

"Tail lights of a car. It was dark colored. Why?" Ted glanced up at Leeland coming down the steps. "Did something happen to Maxine?"

"Yes." He didn't feel like dealing with the gallery owner, or his wife, if they knew Shandra was in danger.

"I think it had Washington plates."

Leeland brushed by. "He's still using the same car. I'll put out a BOLO."

Ted's eyes narrowed. "What's going on?" His gaze followed the captain. "Hey! That's Shandra's Jeep." He started to head that direction.

"Stay here." Ryan strode over to the Jeep and locked the doors. Then he joined Leeland.

In the SUV he leaned back in the seat and took several long breaths.

"We'll find them." Leeland said, pulling away from the curb.

"The only way will be when they call me. And I hope Shandra is still alive."

Chapter Twenty-six

Shandra's shoulders were going numb from the weight of Miranda on top of her. She shifted trying to take some pressure off when the car veered to the right. It felt like they'd stayed on pavement for most of the trip and had crunched over packed snow the last fifteen or twenty minutes.

The vehicle stopped. Doors opened, ushering in cold fresh air. She gulped, hoping it would help revive her numb limbs. The door on her side opened. The weight of Miranda disappeared and she was pulled upright. Before she could get her bearings, she was tossed over a shoulder. It wasn't the smaller man's shoulder.

Hinges and wood creaked as she felt him climb three steps and duck. Musty air and rodent droppings met her nostrils. She dropped onto a cushion and dust drifted into her nose, causing her to sneeze.

The cushion leaned and she toppled onto what had to be Miranda. The other woman squeaked. With the tape over her mouth she couldn't tell her it was an ally laying in her lap.

Hands grasped her shoulders, setting her upright. Something was wedged under her left thigh, keeping her from toppling over again.

"This is a piss poor place to hide out," Devin said.

She could barely hear the whispered reply. The larger man was worried about them recognizing his voice. She hadn't had time to get a good look at him. He'd been dressed in jeans and a sweatshirt. How would the man from Chicago have found a cohort in someone from Huckleberry? And who in Huckleberry that she knew had this man's build? As she flipped through mental images of men she knew, someone outside started chopping wood and someone inside moved furniture.

Sniffling close by told her Miranda wasn't holding up very well. From the bruise on her face, it was apparent the men had been rough with her to get her to make the call. Or possibly when she resisted going with them. Why were they at Maxine's apartment? Was she also in with the local person?

Stomping entered the cabin. She jumped when wood clattered and thumped, making the floor under her feet vibrate.

Soon the smell of wood burning masked the rodent and musty odors. She was still in her coat and fur boots. Her feet were getting warm but she wasn't about to have them removed. If a chance came to get away, she was going to take it.

"Did you find her phone in her purse?" Devin asked.

No reply.

Hands started feeling in her coat pockets. A satisfied grunt echoed in her ear when his hand left the pocket where she'd put her phone.

"We're going to take the tape off your mouth and you're going to tell your lover boy Devin Moore has you and if he doesn't call your number back in two hours, you'll not be as pretty as you are now." Someone grabbed her hair and yanked her head back. Warm minty scented breath rushed across her face. "Understand?"

"Yes." Her mind flashed through how she could give Ryan some clue to where they were. But she didn't have any idea. How far they were from Huckleberry and which direction they went wasn't clear.

The phone pressed against her face.

"Shandra, thank God. Where are you?"

The relief in Ryan's voice started tears sliding down her cheeks.

"Devin M-moore has me. Don't worry— Ow!" Her head jerked back by the yank on her hair.

"Shandra! Shandra!"

She heard desperation in Ryan's voice. "I'm here!" She called back before tape silenced her.

Ryan heard her reply. She was still alive. But for how long.

"Your lady isn't cooperating," Devin said. "If you want her to stay alive call this phone in two hours. I'll tell you what to do then."

Ryan's anger was only rivaled by his fear for Shandra. "Why should I?" The line went dead. He slammed his fist into the wall of the Huckleberry Police Station. The pain in his hand didn't take away the pain in his chest.

"Hey! No destroying government property," Sheriff Oldham said. He, Leeland, two deputies, and six state police all stared at him.

"That was Moore. He has Shandra and told me to call back in two hours." Two hours, there was a lot Moore could do to Shandra in two hours. As a gang member, Ryan had seen what Moore liked to do to women from other gangs. His chest constricted remembering the one girl he'd managed to sneak out and get to a hospital.

"Did he call you from his phone?" Leeland asked.

"No. It was Shandra's…" His brain clicked in. "She allowed me to put GPS tracking on her phone several months ago." He held his phone up and went through the steps to track her phone. Ten agonizing minutes later, he had her phone pinpointed.

"He's holding her about an hour from here out County Road forty-six." He glanced up at the sheriff. "Request permission to accompany you."

Oldham nodded. "But you listen to orders. No running in to save your woman."

He nodded. The last thing he wanted was to put Shandra in any more danger.

~*~

Shandra didn't like the whispering going on across the room. The two were up to something. She didn't know what it was, but it felt like trouble for her and Miranda.

"No!" The masked man raised his voice.

"After hearing her voice, he's going to meet me

wherever I say. Get rid of them. That's what I'm paying you for."

"It'll cost you another fifty grand."

That was the most the masked man had said that she could hear. The voice rang familiar. But who? Where?

"Done," Devin replied immediately.

The order sent a chill down her back.

The sound of ripping tape rang in her ears and her legs parted.

"Get up." A hand grabbed the back of her coat, standing her up.

"And you."

The sound of someone next to her meant he was taking them both out to kill them at the same time. Maybe they had a chance. If she could just get the tape off her mouth, she could...what?

Someone stepped between them. He hooked his arm through hers and started forward. It was either walk or fall on her face.

They went down the steps and to the right and the right again. The snow was a good foot deep. She tried picking her feet up but ended up dragging them through the snow. She heard Miranda breathing heavy on the other side of the man. Her mind flashed to the sight of Miranda in the chair. She had on a nice sweater and nice boots. Like she'd been on a date. Her feet and legs would be freezing by now. Her heart went out to her friend. Shandra hated that the young woman had been drawn into her troubles.

"Stand." The man moved away.

She didn't know which way he went, but her instinct was to try and run. Her legs were tired from the walk, but she willed them to move. Two steps and a gun blast rang out through the woods. She fell into the snow face first. Another round echoed through the trees.

The sound left her ears ringing. Taking an inventory, she didn't find any part of her body injured. She was cold from landing face first in the snow, but she didn't think he shot her. Why?

She rolled to her side and rubbed the edge of the tape on her shoulder, slowly rolling the tape off half of her mouth. "Miranda," she said out of the side of her mouth.

Thrashing to her right had to be the woman.

The next thing was to get sight. She rubbed the side of her face in the snow, slowly working the scarf off her eyes. Her cheek was frozen when the scarf finally rolled off her head. The brilliance of the sun on the snow blinded her. She closed her eyes and slowly raised her eyelids, allowing her eyes to become accustom to the brightness.

She spotted Miranda flopping around in the snow. In a sitting positon, she pushed her way through the snow to the other woman. "Hold still." She leaned backwards, ripping the tape from her mouth.

"Ow!"

"Close your eyes. The sun is a killer after being blindfolded." She grasped the woman's scarf in her fingers and rolled to pull the cloth from her head.

Righting herself, she scanned the trees around them. There wasn't any sign of the man but she could see the tracks they'd made.

"Sit up. I'll pick at the tape on your hands."

"I'm so cold. Why did those men kidnap us?"

Miranda scooted around so their backs were touching.

"They wanted me and used you for bait. I'm bait for them to kill Ryan."

"Why? And why didn't he kill us. That's what they were talking about. Right?"

Miranda's body shook from the cold. Shandra worked as quickly as her cold fingers would, tugging and pulling on the tape, trying to either rip it or find the end.

"Yes. Devin, the redheaded one, wanted us dead. I don't know why ski mask didn't kill us. He was offered good money." She felt the tape give and tugged harder. "Did you recognize the one in the ski mask?"

"Something about him was familiar…But I don't know. I meet so many people at the restaurant it could have been anyone."

The tape gave way.

"Oh!" Miranda scrambled to turn around. She went to work on Shandra's taped wrists.

When they were both free, Shandra offered her coat to Miranda.

"No. If we start walking I'll warm up." She glanced around. "Which way?"

"Not back to where those two are." Shandra pointed the opposite direction of the tracks. "Let's hope we come to a road somewhere out there." she glanced down at the other woman's boots. "I'll break a trail so your feet don't get any wetter." With her fur-lined boots she started dragging her feet, headed what appeared to be east. Hopefully, they would hit a road soon.

Chapter Twenty-seven

Ryan stood back with Sheriff Oldham as the state police and sheriff's deputies surrounded the cabin off County Road 46. Oldham gave the cue and the law men converged on the cabin.

Two shots were fired.

He raced to the building, hitting the steps at a dead run and rushed through the door. Devin Moore lay on the floor, bleeding. Shandra's phone lay on the floor beside him.

"Where is she?" he asked, picking up the phone and staring down at Moore.

His lips twisted into a sneer. "Dead."

Ryan fell to his knees beside the dying man. "She better not be or you'll wish that shot had killed you."

"Ryan! I found tracks!" Leeland called from outside the cabin.

He rushed outside and followed the captain.

"There. Three sets, side by side."

"The women and someone else." He pulled out his Glock and took off as fast as he could go following the tracks. They had to find them alive. His heart and head didn't want to think of any other scenario. His heart pounded in his head as his legs carried him through the snow.

He stopped when the three tracks parted and the snow looked like something had bedded down and rolled around. Catching his breath, he scanned the area.

Leeland caught up to him. "Did you see the set of tracks that went north back there a hundred yards?"

"No. I was focused on the three sets." He walked around the flattened spots. Two scarves and duct tape were colorful spots in the white. A single trail, well-trampled, headed east. "That's got to be them. Come on."

"I'm calling the sheriff about the other tracks and I'll catch up."

He waved and took off at a run following the trail. Twenty-five yards farther, he spotted colors that weren't animals moving through the trees.

"Shandra!" he called and headed toward the movement.

"Ryan!" Her elated reply, made his heart thump even harder than from his running.

"I'm coming!" He continued and spotted Shandra retracing her steps with Miranda following behind her. He'd never seen anything so wonderful in his life.

She ran into his open arms and he held on. He'd thought he'd lost her for good.

"How did you find us?" she asked, wiggling out of

his embrace.

"Remember when I asked if I could put GPS tracking on your phone?"

She stared at him. "Yes. I was humoring you when I agreed. I figured you'd never need to use it."

"That's how we found the cabin. Devin was shot, but not fatally." His mood darkened. "He said you were dead."

"He probably believes we are. He told the other man to kill us. But he shot two times missing us and left us tied up sitting in the snow."

"Who was the other man?" His mind started rifling through Moore's right-hand men.

"We don't know. He wore a ski mask. He was bigger than Devin. He only spoke one word at a time. Like he was afraid we'd recognize his voice." She took hold of Miranda's hands. "We need to get Miranda out of the cold. She's freezing."

He took off his coat and wrapped it around the young woman. She smiled, but her teeth chattered. Holding Shandra's hand, he led them back to the cabin. Leeland met them fifty yards from the cabin.

"I sent deputies after the other tracks. They radioed back the person walked to a campground and looks like he left in a vehicle."

Ryan cursed. "Then we don't know if the threat is gone or not."

Shandra squeezed his hand. "I want to go home and Miranda needs warmed up." She grasped Miranda's hand, leading both her and Ryan toward the cabin. "We'll worry about a continued threat after we're both home."

He had to agree with her there. The women needed

warmed up and to give their statements.

Leeland loaded them into the back of his SUV. Ryan would have preferred sitting in the back with Shandra, but Sheriff Oldham shook his head when he started to get in. He understood they didn't want her statement to include anything Ryan told her.

He was perspiring in the front seat as Leeland kept the heat blasting toward the back to warm the women. They didn't talk, but he heard Miranda and Shandra whispering in the back. They pulled up to the sheriff's office in Warner. Mr. and Mrs. Aducci were standing in front of the building along with his mom and dad. He didn't know how they knew what had happened but it was good to see them standing there.

Miranda slid out of the vehicle and straight into her parent's arms.

Ryan held the door open for Shandra. She slipped out and into his mom's arms. Tears trickled down her face.

Shandra couldn't believe Colleen and Ephraim were at the sheriff's office waiting for her. She collapsed in the older woman's arms as tears burned her eyes.

"There, there. You're safe now," Colleen crooned as a hand rubbed Shandra's back.

"Thank you for being here. It-You don't know what it means." She blinked back the tears as she stared first into Colleen's smiling face and then the older, sterner version of Ryan's face.

"Shandra, we need you to come in and give us your statement," Captain Leeland said, touching her arm.

"Give her a minute," Ryan said, stepping between her and the captain.

She patted Ryan's arm. "It's okay. The sooner I get this done the sooner I can go home." She followed the captain into the building. She heard Ryan and his parents talking as they followed her inside.

Captain Leeland led her into a small room with two soft chairs. On the way in he'd called out to someone to bring in two coffees. She didn't correct him. Anything warm to hold onto would be welcome. Even with the hot air blasting in the vehicle she still felt chilled through and through.

When a young woman in uniform arrived with a cup of coffee and a cup of tea, she smiled. Ryan must have intervened on her behalf.

"I need you to tell me everything that happened and all you can remember about the second man." Captain Leeland pushed a button on a recording machine and picked up his coffee.

She told everything she could remember after receiving Miranda's call.

"Why do you think they used Ms. Aducci to lure you to town?" he asked.

"I honestly don't know. They must have been following me and knew we were friends, but we don't do things together. I only really see her at her family's restaurant. So I don't know why they picked her. I do more things with and see Ruthie Anderson and Naomi Norton more than Miranda."

It was something that nagged at her. Why had they used the young woman to lure her?

"Do you know why they were at Maxine's? Was she in on this?" She didn't want to believe the woman who owned Maxie's would have allowed someone to kidnap her and Miranda.

"She was a victim, too. We found her tied up and gagged in her bedroom when Ryan saw your Jeep outside the bar."

"Good! I didn't want her to be mixed up in this. Did she see the men?"

"They jumped her when she closed the bar and headed to her apartment. Miranda was in the bar that evening. She ordered a drink and disappeared, according to Maxine."

"They must have grabbed her at the bar. But why was she there?" Shandra stared at the officer as if he held all the answers.

"The sheriff is asking her those questions right now." Captain Leeland stood. "You can go home now. If any more questions come up after we compare your statement with Ms. Adduci's I'll call you on Ryan's phone."

She smiled. "Does that mean you're making him take me home?"

The captain smiled. "I think the two of you need some quiet time."

"I couldn't agree more."

She found Ryan and his parents arguing when she entered the lobby.

"We'll be fine going to Shandra's," Ryan said.

"What's wrong?" she asked, walking up beside Ryan.

He rubbed a hand across the back of his neck. A sure sign he was upset. "Mom and Dad think we should spend the weekend with them."

"We're missing the rest of the family," Colleen said. "It would be wonderful to spend time with the two of you."

Shandra could tell Ryan wasn't comfortable with the idea. She didn't know if it was because there was still a person out to get him or because he didn't want to spend that much time with his father.

"How about we come over for Sunday dinner?" she said, hoping it would appease his mother and Ryan.

"That's a wonderful idea! We'll call and have Conor and Lissa over." Colleen pouted. "I wish the others were back. We could make it a real family gathering." She stopped and stared at the two of them. "You both have to come for Christmas mass and spend the night. We'll all be together for the first time in years if you spend Christmas Day with us."

Ryan shook his head. "I don't know…"

"We'll discuss it and let you know on Sunday," Shandra said, hugging Colleen and then Ephraim. She scanned the lobby. Mr. and Mrs. Aducci were watching them.

Shandra crossed the room and hugged them both. "I'm so sorry Miranda was caught up in this."

"You brought her home safe. That's what matters." Mr. Aducci patted her head and Mrs. Aducci nodded.

"I'm leaving. Tell Miranda if she needs to talk to call me." She remembered she didn't have a phone. Ryan stepped up beside her. "I need one of your business cards."

He pulled one out of his wallet and handed it to her.

She tucked it in Mrs. Aducci's hand. "Have her call this number and ask for me if she needs to talk."

"Grazie."

Ryan walked her to the door and pulled her outside. Out on the sidewalk, he pulled her into his arms and kissed her. It wasn't a peck, it was a welcome home and don't ever leave me kiss.

When he came up for air, she gasped and clung to him. "Take me home, my legs aren't going to be able to hold me up much longer."

His parents exited the sheriff's office at that moment.

Chapter Twenty-eight

Ryan remembered his pickup was at Shandra's and her Jeep was in Huckleberry. What he was going to ask would make his mother very happy. "Dad, could you give us a lift to Huckleberry?"

"Oh! We'd be delighted!" Mom hooked her arm through Shandra's and led her toward the car.

"Is everything back to normal?" Dad asked quietly.

"No. There's still someone out there who could want to kill me or kidnap my family or even Shandra again." He wished he could celebrate like his mom suggested, but he didn't see how until this missing person was caught.

"Then it would be best if you don't come to Sunday dinner." Dad slapped him on the back and unlocked the car.

That was his thoughts, too. Unless by some

miraculous luck they discovered the man in the next twenty-four hours.

He slid into the back seat beside Shandra and slipped his arm around her shoulders. His brain was still processing the fact she'd been unharmed while in Moore's hands. He had expected the man to torture her to get back at him.

"What are you thinking?" she whispered and smiled at his mom who peered at them over the front seat.

"Something we'll talk about later."

His mother kept up a chatty conversation as they drove the thirty minutes to Huckleberry.

"Her Jeep is in front of Maxie's," he told his father. Shandra made a face.

"What's wrong?" he asked.

"I don't remember what I did with my keys." She shrugged.

His mom piped up. "We can take you both all the way to Shandra's."

"There's no need." He stuck his hand in his pocket and pulled out his keys. "I have a key for her Jeep with mine."

Shandra hugged him. "That's right. I forgot I gave you the other set and had a new set made to keep at the house."

The car stopped behind the Jeep.

"Thank you both for being at the police station and for driving us here." Shandra grasped his mom's hand and then patted his dad on the shoulder.

"Yeah, thanks. We'll keep you posted on whether we make it Sunday or Christmas." He slipped out of the car before his mom could argue.

Shandra slid out behind him with a questioning look.

"I'll tell you on the way to your place." He unlocked the passenger side door and she climbed in.

He slid behind the steering wheel and started the vehicle. "Hungry?"

"Starving."

"Want to get a burger at Ruthie's or go straight home?" As much as he wanted to get her alone, he also knew she needed to eat.

"It's after lunch. She should be able to whip up a couple of burgers quickly." Shandra rubbed her hands together. "I worked up an appetite making a path for Miranda."

He put the Jeep in gear and headed for the diner. "I wondered why it looked like one of you were dragging your feet. I thought maybe it was to make an easy to follow trail."

"No, Miranda wasn't dressed to be outside. Her boots were thin and her sweater and clothing wasn't warm. It was as if she were dressed for a date."

He glanced over. Shandra stared forward her eyes focused on something inward.

"Who is she dating?"

"I don't know. But you would have thought he would have come forward when she disappeared."

He parked in front of the diner.

Shandra was out of the vehicle and striding through the door before he rounded the hood of the Jeep.

"My favorite couple," Ruthie said, putting an arm around Shandra. "Are you alright?"

Shandra stared at her friend. "How do you know what happened?"

Ruthie tipped her head toward Maxwell sitting at the end of the counter watching her.

"I should have known. I'm fine. Ryan found us and we're safe and getting warm."

"Caramel hot chocolate coming right up," Ruthie said, loud enough for her waitress to hear.

"Thank you. And my usual cheeseburger and sweet potato fries, please."

Ryan put a hand on her back, navigating her to the booth with the heater vent under the table. "I'll have my usual," he called to the cook.

Maxwell didn't wait for them to get settled on the same bench before he slid into the one across from them. "You and Miranda, okay?"

"I'm better than she is. Someone hit her in the face." She shivered thinking about the sweet young woman treated that way.

"We'll get whoever did that to her." Ryan put an arm around her shoulders and stared pointedly at Maxwell. "We're here to eat. Not talk about what happened."

The big man on the other bench, nodded. "How's Sheba doing? Chandler said the wound was healing well."

"She doesn't act like anything happened to her." Shandra smiled. She and her dog were coming out of this in pretty good shape. She leaned her head on Ryan's arm. This whole thing had shown her she was ready to settle down and share her life with someone.

"That's good. Knowing how scared she is of things, I was afraid it would make her even worse." Maxwell sipped the coffee he'd brought with him from the counter.

The waitress set a steaming cup of coffee in front of Ryan and the caramel flavored hot chocolate in front of her.

"Thank you." Shandra wrapped her fingers around the hot beverage and sipped. There had been a few moments after being kidnapped when she'd wondered if she'd get to have these small pleasures again.

The small talk continued and their food arrived. Ruthie slid into the booth alongside Maxwell and they had a normal conversation among friends.

She enjoyed the times the four spent visiting. But it seemed like it was always here at the diner. "Would you two like to come to dinner at my place this next week? Like Monday, when the diner is closed."

Ruthie turned to Maxwell. "Would that work for you?"

He grinned. "It would."

"I'm not sure that's such a good idea." Ryan grasped her hand. "We don't know that the other man will be caught by then."

Shandra huffed out an exaggerated sigh. "We can't live our lives watching every stranger and not enjoying our family and friends."

"I know. I'm not saying we can't have them over. Just, let's wait." He appealed to Maxwell. "How about after the holidays?"

The big man's smile had faded. "That sounds good. Pick a Monday after the holidays and we'll be there."

The bite of the delicious burger wasn't going down as easy now that Ryan had reminded her they wouldn't be free of the threat against him until they captured the man in the ski mask. That thought jogged her brain.

"Sheba brought me a ski mask that she found out in

the woods somewhere." She focused on Maxwell. "Did any of the search and rescue volunteers lose one?"

He shook his head. "Not that I heard of. But I can ask."

"Thanks."

Ryan slid his empty plate to the center of the table and handed Ruthie money. "Let's go. Time to get you home. Your eyelids are drooping."

She knew his tactics. He wanted to get her alone to question her. She sighed and slid out of the booth. Ruthie did too and they hugged.

"It won't be long and you'll have your life back," her friend said.

"I hope so." She released Ruthie and Maxwell hugged her.

"See you soon," he said and winked.

She enjoyed this couple's friendship more than any others she had in Huckleberry. "Count on it."

Ryan escorted her out to the Jeep. They were ten miles from Huckleberry when he asked, "What did you do with the ski mask?"

"I tossed it on top of the dryer."

"I'll bag it as evidence and have someone pick it up. There could be DNA on it that will tell us who it belonged to." He reached over, grasping her hand. "I know you want to get back to normal, but as long as the man who helped Moore kidnap you is still out there, we have to treat him as a threat."

"Even though he didn't shoot us when Devin told him to? That tells me he didn't want to harm us. With Devin caught, why would he go through with killing you?" She'd thought about this on the ride from Warner. With Devin in custody the threat would be over.

"If we can't connect the other deaths to Moore, it means someone else did them. That could be the man who, for whatever reason, let you live."

"Will Devin go free?"

"No, we can press first degree kidnapping charges and because he kidnapped two of you to try and kill a police officer he can get the death penalty or the very least life in prison."

It was a relief to know that threat against Ryan would be gone. "Do you have a way of finding out if any other gangs would be out to kill you?"

He glanced her way. "I have a couple sources who could check things out."

"Good." She leaned her head back on the seat. The warmth and swaying of the vehicle lulled her to sleep.

~*~

At Shandra's place, Ryan pulled up to the front door.

Lil and Sheba hurried out the door. "Is she alright?" the older woman asked, hurrying to the passenger side door.

"She's just asleep." He reached into the vehicle and cradled Shandra in his arms. "I'll put her to bed. Can you stay with her? I'm going to drive back to Huckleberry and check around. There's still a man missing."

"She'd not going to like waking and finding you gone." Lil hurried in front of him, drawing the blankets down on the bed.

"I know, but the sooner we find the other man, the sooner she'll feel safe." He unzipped her coat, pulled her arms from the sleeves, and handed the garment to

Lil.

She tossed the coat to a chair and pulled the boots off Shandra's feet.

Ryan kissed the sleeping woman's forehead and strode out of the room. He was tired and would have rather laid down next to Shandra, but they had to find the man who help Moore. For all they knew he was ready to carry out the gang leader's revenge.

He filled a travel mug with coffee and changed out of his wet boots and socks. When he was ready to leave, he put the ski mask in a plastic bag and headed out to his pickup.

On the way to Huckleberry, he called Whorter and Leeland. They were both meeting him at the Huckleberry P.D. Whorter to get the ski mask and take it to the state forensic lab, and Leeland to let him read the two women's statements.

Chapter Twenty-nine

Shandra woke feeling disoriented, until a wide, wet tongue licked her cheek. She hugged Sheba and rubbed their cheeks.

"I missed you too, girl." She wiggled to a sitting position. Lil sat in a chair by the door, her shotgun across her lap.

"I don't think that's necessary." She pointed to the weapon.

Lil glared at her. "Until that detective of yours says your safe, it's necessary."

"Where is my detective?"

"He took off in his pickup. Something about finding the missing man."

Frustration bubbled. He had to be as tired as she was. He'd get himself killed because he was too rummy to think straight. She couldn't call him. Her cell phone was in police custody.

"Can I borrow your cell phone?" She'd purchased a phone for the woman to keep with her after she'd fallen in the corral and couldn't get up.

"You going to call him and take him away from his business?" Lil didn't make any moves to give her the phone.

"I was going to call and remind him he was up all night just like I was. Two nights in a row is going to make him an easy target for whoever is after him." She shoved Sheba off her and stood.

"I'll go get you some soup. I pulled some out of the freezer right after he left." Lil left the room faster than a cat after a mouse.

Shandra glanced down at the dirty clothes. She headed for the shower.

~*~

In clean sweats and her fuzzy slippers, Shandra wandered out to the kitchen, following the aromas of her own chicken soup. She liked making large batches when she cooked, and freezing them in smaller portions for times when she was busy. Lil had taken to raiding the freezer, too. She not only cooked for her but for her employee.

"Here you go. Homemade soup and that bread you like." Lil set a small plate with slices of the crusty bread Shandra bought at the bakery.

"Thank you." She sat down and started eating.

Lil sat down beside her with a bowl of her own.

"I don't understand how they knew I would come to Miranda's rescue," she said to no one in particular.

"If they'd been watching you, they know you have a big heart." Lil slurped her soup as if to emphasize she

226

wasn't getting mushy.

"How long have they been watching me? Ryan didn't find out there was a threat until after the men were killed." Her head hurt from all the what ifs and whys going around in her mind.

Sheba barked at the front door.

Shandra glanced at the microwave clock. 4:30. Who would be visiting now? Sheba wouldn't bark if she heard Ryan's pickup.

She shuffled her fuzzy slippers into the great room and looked out the window. Mick Sterling stood beside a sedan.

She opened the door. "I thought you went back to Seattle."

He stopped on the front porch. "I had someone else take care of things. I tried to call but you weren't answering your phone, so I thought I'd better come out and check on you."

Sheba pushed up beside her then lunged at the man, growling.

~*~

Ryan sat in the back room of the Huckleberry P.D. reading through Shandra's and now Miranda's statements. He hadn't thought much about her statement that Mick Sterling had called her to meet at Maxie's. Until he got to the end. When Sheriff Oldham asked her if she recognized the man who helped abduct her, she said, his voice sounded familiar.

He picked up his phone and called Lil.

"This is a heck of a time to call!" the snarly woman yelled into the phone.

He heard Sheba in the background growling and Shandra calling her off. "What's going on?"

"That fancy fellow from Seattle showed up and Sheba won't get off him."

His heart froze. "Mick Sterling?"

"Yeah. That guy."

"Shut the door on him and lock all the doors. I'll be there as fast as I can." He grabbed his coat and hollered, "Every available officer to Shandra's. Mick Sterling just showed up and her dog is after him."

~*~

Shandra grabbed Sheba's collar. "Stop! Stop!" Her kind gentle dog had never attacked anyone— human or animal. "I don't understand."

Lil marched past, shoved her inside the house and closed the door, locking it.

"Have you gone crazy! If she harms him, I'll be liable." Shandra tried to get to the door but Lil stood in front of her, her shotgun cradled in her arms.

"Ryan called. He said to shove him out and keep you in."

She stared at the other woman. Ryan thought Mick was the other man. Her mind raced over the impressions the man in the ski mask had given her. She knew him. They'd had dinner at Aducci's. She groaned. She'd all but set up Miranda and Mick. That was how they knew to use the young woman to lure her to them. Her chest squeezed. "If he killed those men, he stabbed Sheba before. What if he…" She couldn't say the words. Her body shook. "We have to get her off him and inside."

Lil leaned around the door and looked out the window. "They're both gone."

Shandra sat down on the arm of the couch. "Do you think he killed her and dragged her away?" She couldn't bear to think of her dog dead.

"Don't see any drag marks. I'd say he is runnin' with her after him. Never seen that dog so mad. I bet he's the one that stabbed her."

"I don't think he had a weapon." A noise behind the house spun her toward the patio.

Mick appeared. He broke the glass door with a rock and lunged into the house.

Sheba sprang through the hole behind him.

He crossed the room headed for Shandra.

She stepped back by Lil who raised her shotgun.

Sheba stood by the hole in the glass door, growling.

The man stopped mid-stride when his gaze landed on the shotgun. He raised his hands. The cold blue eyes she'd witnessed the night she was kidnapped glared at her.

"I should have killed you and that other one." His voice held bitterness.

Sheba growled deeper.

"Why didn't you?" She stayed beside Lil. She knew the woman wouldn't have any qualms about shooting the man should he make a move.

"Because I do like your art and didn't want to kill the person responsible for making such wonderful things." He started to drop his hands.

"No, you don't. Keep them high. The cops is on the way. If you move anything before they get here, I'll claim self-defense. And Shandra here is my witness." Lil tipped her head toward Shanda.

She nodded. There was something else she needed to know. "From the way my usually docile dog is acting, I take it you're the one who killed the marshal and stabbed Sheba."

He stared at her, his mouth clamped tight.

Looked like she wasn't going to get a confession for killing anyone out of him.

"Did you hit Miranda?"

He shook his head. "That was Devin. When she refused to call you, he said she needed some persuasion."

Anger consumed her. "And you let him hit her?"

He shrugged. "You do what you have to do to get results."

"That's the stupidest thing I've ever heard." She started to take a step toward him.

Lil grabbed her sleeve, which made the gun dip.

Mick lunged toward them.

Shandra scrambled toward the couch.

Sheba ran to her.

A boom rang in her ears.

Shandra grabbed Sheba around the neck and called, "Lil! Lil!" She could see purple sticking out from under a still Mick Sterling.

"I'm fine. Can't get this piece of crap off me." It was the first time her indignation sounded rattled.

Officers burst in through all the doors.

They all stopped and stared.

"Don't stand there, get him off Lil!" Shandra shouted.

Ryan jumped over the two bodies and crouched next to her and Sheba. "Are you hurt?"

"No. Lil shot. Is he…" She didn't want to look at Mick.

Ryan raised her to her feet and took her and Sheba into the bedroom. "Stay here until someone comes for your statement."

She was content to stay in the room. "Lil. Make sure she's okay."

"I will. You two stay here." Ryan left the bedroom and stopped beside Leeland. The captain shook his head. Sterling was dead.

He walked over to where Lil was leaning with her arms on the back of a dining chair. "How are you doing?"

Her eyes were wide, her face as white as the snow outside. "I've never shot a person." Her clothing was covered in blood.

"Why don't you go in the guest bathroom and take a shower. I'll bring you some of Shandra's clothes." He touched her shoulder.

She nodded, not giving him any kind of a fight. He watched her stagger down the hall to the guest bath.

"They tell you anything?" Sheriff Oldham asked.

"No. I'm going to get some clothes for Lil. Why don't you follow me into Shandra's bedroom. You can take her statement." He waved a hand. "I don't want her to see this."

Oldham nodded and followed him. He opened the door.

"Lil? How is she?" Shandra stood up off the bed.

"She's taking a shower. Want to give me some clothes for her to put on when she gets out?"

Shandra scurried around her room. She clutched sweats and warm socks. "I'll take these to her and make some tea."

He put an arm out stopping her. "No. You stay here. Sheriff Oldham wants to take your statement. I'll bring Lil in here when she's done, and I'll bring in some tea." Ryan turned to the sheriff. "Keep her in here."

He nodded.

Ryan kissed Shandra's cheek. "I'll be right back."

Shandra stared at the closed door. She whipped her gaze to the sheriff. "What doesn't he want me to see?"

He cleared his throat. "A shotgun makes a mess."

She thought about that a moment and shuddered.

"Sit." He sat in the chair Lil had occupied earlier.

Shandra sat on the bed. Sheba shoved her head into her lap. She stroked the dog's fur as she relayed everything that happened from the time Mick arrived.

"Will Lil be in trouble for-for killing him?" She didn't want to see her friend in jail for protecting her. "She did it to save me."

"No. It was self-defense. We know he was one of the men who abducted you, he was a threat to you." Sheriff Oldham closed his book. He leaned forward. "I hope all this mess hasn't scared you away from Ryan. He's been a happier person since he's met you."

She smiled. After all that had just happened she knew that smile came from knowing Ryan. "Sheriff, he's done the same for me."

He stood and the door opened.

Ryan shuffled Lil into the room.

Shandra sprang off the bed and hugged the older, smaller woman. "Thank you," she whispered in the woman's ear.

Lil nodded and sat down on the bed when Shandra pulled her down beside her.

Sheriff Oldham sat back down as Ryan returned with a tray of cookies, tea, and coffee. He sat on the other side of Shandra as the sheriff took down Lil's statement.

When Lil came to the point where she pulled the trigger, the woman's body shuddered.

Shandra put an arm around her. "You did what had to be done. You saved us."

Her green eyes narrowed. "No one messes with my family."

"That's right." Shandra hugged the woman and smiled at Ryan.

Chapter Thirty

Shandra had spent the past week at Ryan's house in Warner while Lil oversaw the cleaning crew at her house. They'd learned Mick Sterling was an alias and the M.O. he'd used to kill the Deputy U.S. Marshal and the other man was the same used on several hits on the west coast.

Her phone jingled. The screen showed Naomi Norton.

"Hi Naomi, Merry Christmas Eve," Shandra answered.

"Thanks. You too. Hey, I'm calling because you know the check went through on the sale of your art to Mr. Sterling."

"Yes." She hadn't even thought about the fact the man Lil had killed had bought her art.

"Well, the check cleared and now the crated art

came back." The question in her voice mirrored Shandra's thoughts.

"You have art work that has been paid for." Without hesitation, she knew what to do. Ryan had checked Mick's real background, and he didn't have any family that would be looking for the art or wondering where the money had gone.

"We have two choices; we can give the money to a charity and resell the art, or I can give the art pieces to a charity to sell." And she knew which charity it would be.

"I'll give you a check the next time you come to town. And some charity is going to be very lucky. Have fun with Ryan's family." Naomi ended the conversation.

Shandra smiled. Her excitement over the gift to the charity made her giggle.

Ryan walked in the room. "What's so funny?"

"Not funny, exciting. And you'll have to wait until tomorrow." She kissed his cheek and went back to putting packages in a box.

Today was Christmas Eve and they had agreed to go to mass with Ryan's family. Once his sisters learned the threat was gone, they'd returned home. She was not only going to have Christmas with Ryan, but his whole family. She'd never had a large family Christmas.

She'd spent the day before traipsing all over Warner to purchase presents for all of his family. He wanted to go with her, but she'd insisted on doing it on her own. Now they were packing to spend the night at his parents' house.

"I don't understand why you told my mom we'd spend the night. I only live thirty minutes from their house. We could have woke up early tomorrow and still beat Conor and Lissa there." Ryan dropped his duffel bag on the floor by the front door. All the presents she'd bought and wrapped were in two big boxes on the other side of the door.

"Because it made your mom happy." She placed her small overnight bag next to his duffel.

"What about my dad?" He raised an eyebrow.

"I'm sure he's happy as well. They both say they don't see you enough." She twirled away as his arms came out to grab her.

"I think you like the idea of having a big family." He opened the door. "Wait until tomorrow when everyone starts asking you all kinds of questions. You'll be ready to head for the hills, just like me." He picked up a box and carried it out to her Jeep.

~*~

Shandra couldn't believe the amount of noise five kids, ten adults, and three dogs could make. The squealing became high pitched when Colleen opened her present from Conor and Lissa and it had a photo of an ultrasound in it.

It was going to be hard to top giving Colleen another grandchild but Shandra walked over and handed her card to Ryan's mother.

"What's this?" Colleen turned the card over and gazed up at Shandra.

"It's a gift for your charity." Her cheeks heated as all the adults turned their attention on her.

Colleen opened the card and read the inside. "This is too generous."

She shook her head. "The story behind the money is a long story. One I'll tell later when the kids are in bed."

"It's still generous." Colleen stood and hugged her. "If you don't do something soon to make sure this woman doesn't get away, I'll have to evoke my mother privileges," Ryan's mother said, wagging her finger at her youngest son.

Ryan grinned. "We're working on it."

Everyone cheered and went back to helping children with their presents.

Shandra eased her way out of the chaos and leaned against the doorway to the living room.

Ryan walked up beside her. His arm came around her and he said in her ear, "I told you the noise would drive you crazy."

"It's a good noise." She leaned back against him. "I could put up with this a couple times a year."

"Good. Now that the threat to me is gone, I plan on hanging out with my family more." He kissed her temple. "And I'm dragging you along to suffer with me."

They both laughed, but she knew even though they loved their peace and quiet. The noise of a family would never grow old.

Colleen rushed around the room, handing out small glasses with a clear liquid to all the adults. She held hers up. "To my family. May we always have time for a good chat, a good quarrel, and a good laugh. Merry Christmas!"

Everyone downed the fiery liquid and replied, "Merry Christmas."

About the Author

Thank you for joining Shandra, Ryan, and Sheba in another mystery. If this is the first Shandra Higheagle Mystery you've read, please check out the other six books in this series. ***Double Duplicity***, ***Tarnished Remains***, ***Deadly Aim***, ***Murderous Secrets***, ***Killer Descent***, and ***Reservation Revenge***. While each one is stand alone, Shandra and Ryan's romantic arc can be seen through the progression of the series.

If you enjoyed this book, please leave a review. It is the best way to repay an author for your hours of entertainment and their months of writing the book.

I love to hear from fans. You can contact me through my website, blog, or newsletter. My newsletter only comes out when I have a new book or special for my fans. I also have a review team who receive ARCs. You can also find me on Goodreads, Facebook, and Pinterest.

All my work has Western or Native American elements in them along with hints of humor and engaging characters. My husband and I raise alfalfa hay in rural eastern Oregon. Riding horses and battling rattlesnakes, I not only write the western lifestyle, I live it.

Paty
Murder Mystery & Western Romance starring Cowboys and Indians.
www.patyjger.net

Shandra Higheagle Mystery Series

Double Duplicity

Tarnished Remains

Deadly Aim

Murderous Secrets

Killer Descent

Reservation Revenge

Contemporary Action Adventure Romance

Secrets of a Mayan Moon

Secrets of an Aztec Temple

Secrets of a Hopi Blue Star

Secrets of a Christmas Box

Windtree
Press

Thank you for purchasing this Windtree Press
publication. For other books of the heart, please visit
our website at www.windtreepress.com.

For questions or more information contact us
at info@windtreepress.com.

Windtree Press
www.windtreepress.com

Hillsboro, OR 97124

Made in the USA
Columbia, SC
09 November 2022

70707102R00133